Bitter Isolation

Misty Hollow, Book 6

Cynthia Hickey

ISBN: 978-1-956654-59-2

DEDICATION

To those eagerly awaiting the next book.

Chapter One

Shea Sydney should have waited until morning to make the drive, but the anticipation of finally exacting revenge for her father's death spurred her into the bitter cold night. If the moving truck hadn't been running late, she wouldn't be out at this time of the night trying to see through blinding snow. Not to mention the heater in her older model car decided to stop working an hour back.

Shea trembled so hard her teeth clattered. She turned the windshield wipers to full speed and leaned forward to see through the frozen window to the road. The weather grew worse the further up the mountain she drove.

Snow mixed with ice pelted the front windshield, reminding her of the spaceship zooming through the galaxy in Star Wars. Should she pull over until the storm let up, or should she turn around and go home? Her rental house wouldn't have furniture until the movers delivered her things tomorrow anyway.

No, she'd come this far. Another mile or two, and she'd be headed down into the valley of Misty Hollow.

At a snail's pace, she continued. Hope sprang as the road curved downward. The worst of the drive was behind her in this wintery hell.

Her car slid sideways, slowly at first, then began to pick up speed. Shea's heart beat in her throat.

A dark shape loomed ahead then came closer.

Her grip tightened on the steering wheel so hard her knuckles ached.

She closed her eyes right before impact.

The jolt slammed her head into the back of her seat, then jerked forward.

She sat there a moment, her breathing coming in quick gasps, and assessed her condition. She didn't appear to be injured, thanks to her seatbelt. It looked as if a new car was now a necessity. Even a minor accident would have finished off this vehicle.

She climbed from the car to see what she'd hit. A frigid wind whipped up the back of her coat and down the neckline. She crossed her arms tight around her middle. She'd hit a parked truck.

The vehicle sat a weird angle. Shea trudged to the closest side and peered in the window. Thank God, it was empty. A jack that must have fallen when the collision occurred lay in the snow. Where was the driver? Thinking he or she must have gotten a ride out of the storm, she turned back to her car.

A pair of denim-clad legs stuck out of the ditch. Shea scrambled down to find a man. Was this the driver? The man was lucky. A few more feet and he'd have fallen over the cliff, and she wouldn't have seen him at all. Was he even alive?

She dropped to her knees in the snow, took off her glove, and felt for a pulse. Strong and steady. Shea needed to call for help. Slipping and sliding her way back up to her car, she fished around on the floor for her cell phone. No service. Her eyes darted up and down the road. Other than her car and the man's truck, she hadn't seen another vehicle since driving up the mountain.

With a groan, she returned to the man and fought to get him up. "Come on." At over six feet, he was too large for her to manage on her own. Shea returned once again to her car and retrieved the sleeping bag she'd be using that night and placed it over him. She sat on a rock and huddled into a ball to keep warm, praying for someone to drive by.

"What the…" The man sat up, tossing aside her sleeping bag. "Who are you?"

At the sound of the man's voice, she bolted up. "Shea Sydney. My car slid into your truck."

"Yeah," he winced. "I remember that. I jumped back as my truck slid from the jack. I must have hit my head." His eyes narrowed. "Why are you sitting out here in the snow?"

"I couldn't leave you." She pushed stiffly to her feet. "Please tell me you have a way of finding us help."

"If I did, I wouldn't be changing a tire during a snowstorm." He picked up the sleeping bag. "Looks like we're walking off this mountain. This ought to keep us warm."

Her eyes widened. "As in share?"

"Unless you want to freeze." He wrapped half around him, covering his head, and held the other half open. "Well?"

"Are you fit enough to walk?"

"I've a thick skull. Come on."

She grabbed her purse from the car and slipped

under the bag. The man's body heat immediately dispelled the chill in her bones.

"I'm Zeke Matchett."

She stiffened at hearing his name. Could he be related to the man she sought? Forcing herself to remain calm, she said, "Nice to meet you. I'm sorry about all this."

"Luckily you weren't going very fast when you hit that black ice." He wrapped his arm around her waist as she slipped.

"Yeah. Lucky." She stepped out of his hold. It wouldn't do to become too friendly with a possible relative of a murderer.

~

"How far until we reach town?" Shea asked.

"Five miles, but it's a windy road. Ever hear the saying about a country mile?" Zeke grinned, wishing he could see her face better. From the glimpse he caught of her face through the snow, she looked like a beauty with dark hair, a thin build, and a soft voice. "What brings you to town?"

"I'm the new deputy at the sheriff's department."

He'd bet she was the best-looking deputy he'd ever seen. "I own Matchett Winery. We'll reach my place before town. You're welcome to crash there until we can call for a ride out to retrieve our vehicles."

"The moving truck will be at my place bright and early."

"Not if the storm continues."

"Okay. Thank you for the offer." She sounded reluctant.

He gave a mental shrug. "No one will think anything bad about you staying at my place. It's big enough for you to have your own space. Where will you be living?"

She gave him the address.

"That house is pretty secluded. Backs up to my grapevines. You sure you want to stay there alone?"

"I like my privacy. Plus, the rent is cheap."

They made the rest of the walk in silence. The cold deepened, stealing his breath. The sight of a light through the window of his house had never been more welcome. "Look down there. That's my place. We'll turn left at the iron gate."

"Thank God. I think my eyes are frozen open."

He chuckled and pushed open the gate. They'd reach the main house in ten minutes.

When they did, he shook the snow from the sleeping bag and unlocked the front door. Inside, he hung the sleeping bag over a chair and headed to the fireplace. "Make yourself at home. The guest bedroom is down the hall, second door on your left, the bathroom first door on the left. Once I have a fire going, I'll make some hot chocolate, or would you prefer something stronger? I've beer in the fridge and whiskey in the cupboard."

"Hot chocolate sounds wonderful." She removed her coat.

Yep, she was as pretty as he thought with hair the color of dark chocolate, a hint of red under the light, and bright blue eyes.

Once he had a fire going, he headed to the kitchen to make the hot chocolate with milk, the way his mother had taught him. By the time he'd finished, Shea had joined him, her hair tied back.

"I should have brought my suitcase."

"You'd have hated lugging it down the mountain, and the rollers wouldn't have worked in the snow. I can lend you something if you don't mind it being baggy."

"At this point, I don't mind."

"Watch the milk so it doesn't scald. I'll be right back." He rushed to his room where he changed into dry clothes. Minutes later, he handed Shea a pair of drawstring pajama bottoms and a long-sleeved tee shirt.

Soon, they each chose an end of the sofa and sipped on their hot chocolates.

"You'll like Misty Hollow," he said.

She arched a brow. "Really? This town has been in the news a lot over the last year. Seems like there's a lot of crime to me."

"Not so much. You don't hear about the good things. As isolated as this town is, it's a good place for people to hide, but it's also a great place to live."

"The crime is why Sheriff Westbrook hired me without a face-to-face interview. Everything was done over video chat." She blew on her drink.

He couldn't argue that. The town had needed more law enforcement for a while now. "You must have a good record."

"I do." She smiled, sending his heart somersaulting. "Who's the men in the picture on the mantel?"

"My father and his two brothers, Buford and Buck. They're twins. Buck died a few years ago, leaving me this vineyard. Buford lives higher on the mountain and stays pretty much to himself."

"This is a big place for you alone."

"True, but it's where my dad and his brothers were raised. Someday, I hope to fill it with a family of my own." Once he found the right woman anyway.

"What does the surviving uncle do?"

"He has a share in the winery. Uncle Buford used to

be mayor of Misty Hollow years ago." Zeke left off the fact his uncle now drank too much and rarely left his home except to go to the bar.

Her gaze remained on the photo. Even from where he stood, he saw her features harden before she lifted the mug to her lips.

Suspicion rose. Why the interest in his family? It's almost as if she knew about his uncles before arriving. Had Buford wronged her or her family in some way? It wouldn't be the first time. The man had made a lot of enemies during his time as mayor and even more afterward.

"I'm ready for bed. I'll give you a ride to your place in the morning." He rose to his feet and carried both mugs to the kitchen where he set them in the sink.

"Thank you again, Zeke."

"No problem." He forced a smile to his face. "Sleep well." There was no way he would even think of getting to know this woman until he discovered the real reason she was here.

Because messing with Buford meant trouble.

Chapter Two

The next morning Shea bolted upright in the bed until she remembered the events of the night before. She'd almost killed a man while driving through a snowstorm she shouldn't have been driving in and was now without a vehicle. Her arrival in Misty Hollow left a lot to be desired.

Add in the fact she was under the roof of the nephew of the very man she intended to make pay for killing her father. With a heavy sigh, she tossed off the thick quilt and slid from the bed.

Her clothes, now dried and folded, lay on a chair. Had she really slept so soundly that she hadn't heard Zeke enter the room? Shea glanced at the nightstand where her gun rested. She very well could've killed him, if he'd startled her awake.

Shaking her head, she changed into her own clothes and found her way to the kitchen where Zeke flipped pancakes. "Thank you for drying my clothes."

"You're welcome." He turned from the stove with a grin. "Hope you like omelets. I've already called for a tow truck. They'll meet us at the wreck with two trucks in about an hour."

"You have something else to drive?"

"Sure. I only use that old truck when I'm hauling things. I drive a Mercedes Roadster."

Of course, he did. The size of the house and the tasteful furnishings showed Mr. Zeke Matchett had money. Or at least somebody in his family did. "Know where I can rent or buy cheap?"

"I can lend you a car, Shea. I have a couple."

"No, I'm not very lucky with cars. I'd hate for something to happen." It wasn't a good idea to be any more in this man's debt than she already was.

"The local mechanic always has vehicles for sale. He started selling when he took over the place about eight months or so ago. He'll take your old car in trade for a few dollars. Then, he'll turn around and sell it to a junkyard. Makes a pretty penny for himself." Zeke set an omelet with cheese, bacon, and spinach in front of her. "I'll run you by there."

"Thank you." Another thing for him to do for her. After that, she wouldn't let him do a thing. "I have to meet the movers first." She glanced at her watch. "In less than an hour is their predicted arrival time.

He sat across from her with an omelet of his own. "That's fine. I'm not very busy in the winter." Zeke smiled, faint creases showing around eyes as dark as his hair. Almost black, his hair shone under the chandelier. A very handsome man, Zeke Matchett. He was also too nice, which made her suspicious. No one could be both handsome and nice. At least, she'd never met anyone like that.

After a quick breakfast, Shea donned her coat, slipped her gun back into her purse, and met Zeke in the living room. "I really do appreciate this."

"Hey, I need to get my truck, too." He flashed

another grin. "I'm yours all day if you need me."

Lord.

Thankfully, the storm had abated. A clear blue sky contrasted beautifully with the fresh snow that looked as if someone had scattered a fine glitter over everything.

Zeke drove them to the crash site where two tow trucks were already loading the vehicles onto their trucks. "Do you need anything out of your car?"

"Everything in the trunk." Her suitcase and the case files pertaining to her father's death. Those she didn't trust leaving with the movers.

Zeke helped her onto the tow truck to retrieve her belongings then loaded them in the back of his vehicle. The rumble of a motor caught her attention. The moving truck passed them, the driver tossing her a wave. Good. She could find another car in a couple of hours and start doing what she came here for.

As the tow trucks pulled away, Shea and Zeke returned to his Mercedes and headed for her rental. The red brick house with a porch that stretched across the front and one side looked as sweet as it had in the photo online. And, since Misty Hollow was secluded with few amenities, rent was cheap.

With her and Zeke's help, the moving truck emptied quickly, and Zeke drove her to town. As they descended the hill, Zeke told her how the town acquired its name.

"My friend and his wife have the perfect place to watch the mist dissipate. I'll take you up there sometime." He smiled. "It's a sight you won't forget."

She mumbled and stared out the window. Shea did not want to watch the sun rise with this man. If he were anyone else, then absolutely. But a Matchett? No.

The trucks pulled into the lot of a mechanic. A burly

man in dark coveralls approached them, spoke to the drivers, then approached Zeke and Shea. Zeke rolled down his window.

"Hey, Zeke. Looks like you were in a bit of an accident," the man said.

"Yeah, Jo. This lady slid on some ice and hit the truck while I was changing a tire."

"I'll fix it up. Should I bill her insurance company?"

Shea's eyes widened. She hadn't thought of giving Zeke her information. "I'm so sorry." She fumbled in her purse.

"We didn't even call the authorities, Jo. I'll take care of the bill."

"No, Zeke." What was he doing? "Keep whatever this man gives me for my car."

"Don't be silly. Jo, what will you give her for the car?"

Jo frowned. "I guess I could give her five."

It was better than nothing. Shea held out her hand. "Done. I need another car. My name is Shea Sydney, the new deputy."

"Well, why didn't you say so?" Jo rocked on his heels. "I'll give you a great deal. Come on. I have three you can look at. I make sure they're in tip-top shape before selling them."

That made her feel better. She slid out of the car and followed Jo around the building. Zeke parked the car and joined them.

Shea had her choice of a Chevy Impala, a Toyota Corolla, and a two-year-old Toyota Tacoma four-wheel drive. "I want the Tacoma. Do you take payments?"

"Sure do. Come with me, and we'll get you fixed up." Jo led them into his office.

Shea smiled. The truck would allow her to go places a car wouldn't. She'd gladly make payments for a reliable vehicle.

~

Zeke had recognized the boxes he'd put in his car as the ones law enforcement kept case notes in. Everything in him suggested he open one and see who the files were on. If she was looking into his uncle, it would have to be done very carefully. Even family wasn't safe from his uncle's wrath when he got angry. Zeke doubted the pretty new deputy could stand up to Buford.

Zeke shrugged. He'd done the gentlemen thing by letting her sleep in his guest room and being her taxi driver. They most likely wouldn't see each other again besides a casual passing on the street.

After she signed the papers and received her key, Shea stared up at him. "Thank you."

"You're welcome." The corner of his lips twitched at her formality. Uh-oh. Speaking of the devil. Buford drove into the lot.

"What's wrong?" Shea followed his gaze. From the stony look that crossed her face, his uncle's presence was not a good thing.

It also supported his theory that Shea had another reason besides being a deputy in Misty Hollow. His uncle climbed from his big, tired truck and marched their way. No coat, cowboy boots, a baseball cap, and a cigarette dangling from his lips, the big man could be very intimidating.

"I heard about your accident," Buford said, his breath smelling of whiskey. "You all right?"

"Just a fender bender. I'm fine."

"You the little lady that almost killed my nephew?"

Shea hitched her chin, standing only about three inches shorter than his uncle. She sniffed and frowned. "Yep."

"Looks like the new lady deputy needs to take driving lessons." Buford crossed his arms.

"Black ice," Zeke said. "It's all good."

His uncle grunted. "Lucky for the deputy." He lumbered toward his truck.

"You should not be driving under the influence," Shea called out.

"Try and stop me." He climbed into his truck, tipped his cap at her, and sped away.

"Wait until I'm actually working. Thanks again, Zeke." She strolled toward her new truck then stopped. "How do I get to the nearest grocery store?"

"It isn't fancy, but there's one at the end of Main Street. Out of the lot here, turn left and drive until you reach the town's one stoplight. That's Main Street. Turn right again. Good luck."

He slid into his car and watched as she climbed into her truck. How long until Shea and Buford butted heads, and his uncle started making things difficult for her? His uncle had ways of getting to a person without any suspicion falling on himself.

If it reached the point Shea's life was in danger, Zeke would also have to risk his own. He couldn't let his uncle harm another person. Buford had probably killed his own brother, Buck, but Zeke couldn't prove it. Not yet, anyway. Buck had been in too good of shape to become weak and fall, hitting his head on the corner of the table.

Zeke drove home, his heart skipping a beat to see Buford's truck in front of his house. He took a deep breath then exhaled heavily. Zeke wasn't in the mood to deal with his uncle who would want to know every single detail of the previous day. Pulling into the garage, he cut the engine. No sense stalling. Buford would wait however long it took.

"Didn't expect to see you today," Zeke said, entering the living room.

Buford held a crystal glass, twirling it to see the light through the whiskey inside. "Don't be weak over a pretty face, boy. The woman was in the wrong."

"She apologized about the accident." He shed his coat and sat across from his uncle. "The truck is fine, and I'm fine."

"You could have been killed, boy! Then I'd have to run this place, and I don't want anything but my share of the profits."

"But, I didn't." He met his uncle's unflinching eyes and copied. There were two stubborn men in this room.

"Fine." He waved the hand not holding the glass. "Whatever. You keep not holding folks accountable, and it will be your downfall someday. Especially with those in law enforcement who think they lord it over everyone." He downed the whiskey and pushed to his feet. "Remember that." He left, leaving the door open.

"They do not." Zeke stood and closed the door against the winter chill. Buford's share was only a quarter. Buck and Zeke's father had owned the rest. His uncle did nothing for that twenty-five percent except hold out his hand when there was a profit.

He washed the dishes from breakfast and headed to his office. While he needed to work on the books, he googled Shea instead.

She'd been in law enforcement for five years. Her

father, an ex-cop, had been shot execution-style while responding to a domestic disturbance. The address was one Buford and Sybil had lived in before returning to Misty Hollow.

The interrogation of his uncle and aunt had revealed that, yes, things had become heated, but it wasn't until a masked gunman came on the property that the real shouting began. When Detective Sydney had arrived, the gunman had shot him in the back of the head and fled. Authorities had believed the story.

Zeke leaned back in his chair, hands folded behind his head. Since Shea had come to Misty Hollow when she could have gone anywhere, he surmised she didn't believe the facts of the night her father had died.

Shea was here for Buford, and that was very bad.

Chapter Three

Shea slept surprisingly well in her new home. It made a difference sleeping on her own mattress surrounded by familiar things. She hadn't stayed awake thinking about Buford Matchett either, which also surprised her. A traumatic night and nonstop day proved to be the best sleeping aid.

Dressed in dark pants with matching blazer and a blue blouse, she climbed in her Tacoma and drove to the first day of her new job. With a deep breath, she squared her shoulders and marched into the building. A middle-aged woman sat at the reception desk.

"I'm Shea Sydney, the new deputy."

"I'm Doris Belwright. Nice to meet you. I'll ring the sheriff." She picked up her phone. "He'll be here in a minute. Have a seat."

Shea preferred to stand and occupied herself flipping through fliers of the state's most wanted. She turned at the sound of footsteps.

A handsome blond man, maybe ten years older than herself, smiled as he approached. "Nice to see you, Deputy Sydney. I'm Sheriff Westbrook. Come on back, and I'll introduce you to the other deputy, Graham O'Connor."

They paused in the doorway of a room with two desks. "Deputy O'Connor, meet Deputy Sydney. The two of you will share this office." He jerked his head to a room opposite that one.

In his office, the sheriff waved her into a chair and slid some papers across the desk for her to fill out. "Once that's done, I'll give you your badge and weapon. We've had complaints of someone messing around an old barn just outside of town. It'll be a good way to start for you. O'Connor will go with you." He leaned back in his chair. "Have you met anyone in town yet?"

She told him of her accident. "So, the two Matchett men and Jo, and that's it, other than the people in this building."

"It's a small town. You'll know everyone pretty soon."

If she stayed long enough. Once she proved Buford killed her father and the man was locked up, she'd be returning to Little Rock.

She finished the paperwork, received her badge and gun, and went to the other office. "I'm ready."

Graham rose to his feet. "I'll drive." He flashed a grin, grabbed keys from a hook near the door, and led her out a back door to a squad car. "It isn't far."

She buckled her seatbelt. "Misty Hollow has seen a lot of crime lately, hasn't it?"

"I'm fairly new, too, but yes, from what I've heard and read. It's a good place for people to hide, but it's also a good place for people to live."

"Sounds like an oxymoron."

"Even small towns have crime. Evil is everywhere." He backed from the parking spot and drove out of town.

The barn they were sent to looked ready to fall

down. She'd seen several houses and barns falling into ruin. Why weren't they torn down before reaching such a state? The sight made her sad at the lack of love for something that someone had once been proud of.

As soon as she stepped through the hanging door, she could tell drug abusers had been using the barn. Several sleeping bags lay on the ground around a mirror, a candle, and some assorted dishes. Gutted ink pens littered the dirt floor. Beer cans and liquor bottles were scattered around the place. A hypodermic needle and a razor blade sat on a plate.

"Short of staking the place out, we won't be able to keep anyone from coming back," she said.

"We can make them have to replace their belongings." He started rolling everything into a sleeping bag.

"Is that even legal?" Her brow arched.

"What do you want to do with all this? We don't know who left these things. They'll definitely come back if we leave everything." He huffed. "Okay, I've a notebook in the car. Leave them a note that we'll be coming by unannounced and for them to vacate the premises."

That should work. She wrote the note and stuck it on a nail near the door. "What now?"

"We cruise Main Street."

She laughed. "Like kids?"

"Except we're allowed to drive back and forth." He tossed the things in the back of the truck. "We'll bag all this as evidence in case we get lucky and find out who they belong to."

She glanced at her watch. Hours to go before she could start combing through the evidence of her father's death. But, she needed an income in order to stay, so work it had to be.

Cars lined both sides of Main Street. Whether employees working in the shops or customers, she couldn't tell, but the scene resembled something from a Hallmark movie. There was no such thing as drop-dead gorgeous men sweeter than sugar who lived in idyllic towns. Both the men and the town could hold secrets, some very bad ones. She wouldn't allow herself to fall into the trap of Zeke or this place.

Speaking of the devil. She spotted Zeke entering the local drugstore with a case of wine.

"Matchett Winery is a favorite around here. It's good stuff," Graham said. "Zeke is always working on new recipes."

She made a noncommittal sound but tossed an obligatory wave when Graham tapped the horn and Zeke turned. "Don't be surprised if you find a bottle in a welcome basket at your door. He's a nice guy."

"So, I've heard." She sighed.

Shea did indeed have a gift basket waiting for her back at the office. A bottle of red wine, a bottle of white, some chocolates, and a small bouquet of daisies. She rolled her eyes and sat at her desk to fill out the report on the barn.

~

After making the few deliveries, Zeke dropped off a welcome basket at the sheriff's department. He'd done the same for Graham when he'd arrive a few months ago.

When he arrived home, his truck sat in the driveway, a new tire in place of the old, and the keys in the ignition. Zeke parked the Mercedes then removed the keys from the truck. He preferred driving the heavier vehicle on the mountain roads. Less likely to total the vehicle if he hit a deer. Plus, he didn't like flaunting his wealth around town.

Unlike his uncle who stormed through the front door in cowboy boots that cost more than most people made in a week. "Time to check the books." Something he did once a month.

Zeke had begun thinking his uncle wanted to find out if he'd messed up somewhere. "You know where everything is."

"Darn right. I grew up in this house." His boots thudded the wooden floorboards as he headed for the office. "When are you going to hire a full-time housekeeper?"

"I don't need one." He didn't mind cleaning.

"O'Ryan's wife still cleans houses."

"As I said, I don't need one." He exited the house to meander around the dormant grapevines. When the grapes were ripe, the scene was a gorgeous one. He even liked the brown stalks against the white snow. These vines had served his family well for many years. Wandering among them did the best at calming him and was preferable to staying in the house with Buford.

He spotted Shea's house at the end of his property and turned to leave when she appeared from the side of the house lugging firewood. Without a thought, Zeke ran over to her. "Let me do that for you." Why did she look aggravated to see him?

"I've got it."

"Then at least let me cut some wood for you. The landlord should have made sure you were stocked." He headed for the axe imbedded in a stump, not taking no for an answer.

Most people responded kindly to his offers of help. Why not Shea?

"Are you so bored you roam the vineyard searching for someone to help?" She shook her head and put the wood in the house before coming to stand next to him. "Because that's what it seems like to me."

"My uncle is there, so I'd rather not be." He whacked a chunk of wood in two.

"Why not?"

"You met him. Why do you think?" Another whack into a second piece.

"Because he's arrogant and rude?"

"Something like that."

She stared at him for a moment then returned to the house.

Zeke continued to work until he had enough wood split to last her a few weeks. He watched her for a moment through the back-door window. Papers were strewn across the table. When she caught him looking, she turned one over and waved him in.

"I've put coffee on if you want a cup. There are some cookies in the oven. Chocolate chip oatmeal. Thank you for the wood."

"Let me know when you start to get low. Splitting wood keeps me in shape." He poured a cup of coffee and sat across from her. "Working on a case?"

"Cold case. I'm trying to prove my suspicions of who killed my father."

"Any ideas?"

The corner of her lip curled. "I've a very strong suspicion. That's why I'm in Misty Hollow."

How much digging did he need to do before she'd tell him she suspected Buford? "I hope you find your proof."

"Oh, I will. That I guarantee." She smiled over the rim of her cup.

The cookies filled the room with a delectable aroma. Zeke's stomach growled, reminding him he'd missed lunch. Eating with his uncle would rob a man of his appetite faster than anything.

Shea removed the cookies from the oven. A few minutes later, a plateful sat in the middle of the table, and the papers she'd been working on were pushed to the side. "Is coffee still okay, or would you like a glass of milk?"

"Coffee is fine." He reached for a warm, gooey cookie and almost moaned in bliss at the first bite. "Delicious."

A smile teased her lips. "I like to bake, especially when I'm stressed or deep into a case."

"That's why I walk the vineyards no matter the weather. It relaxes me." He studied the lines of her face, the softly curved cheeks, full lips that were a mix of a bit of a pout and some hardness. This woman had seen rough times if her sometimes-sharp gaze meant anything. "Any family?"

Sadness shadowed her features. "Just me after my father was murdered ten years ago. You?"

"Just Uncle Buford." Lucky him. "As I told you before, his twin, Buck, left me the vineyard. While I have the controlling share, Buford still likes to look over my shoulder to make sure I'm doing everything to his satisfaction."

"Rankles, doesn't it?"

"Like a tick in a spot you can't reach." He chuckled. "I like you, Shea Sydney. You're a good person, and I have a sixth sense about people." He stood and held out his hand. "Welcome to Misty Hollow. May you find what you're looking for."

"Oh, I will." A hard glint shone in her eyes despite the smile on her lips. "Again, thank you for the wood."

He nodded and left, heading across the vine fields with long strides to keep warm. He frowned at the sight of his uncle's vehicle still in the drive. More than likely, he'd want to go over the numbers with Zeke and complain about the expenses same as always. The man liked his liquor and hated anything that reduced the amount of funds going into his pocket.

"Good thing you don't want to hire a housekeeper," Buford growled from his chair. "You're spending too much money as it is."

"We're in the black, Uncle. We're doing better than we projected we would this year."

"Those new grapes aren't going to be ready for three more years."

"And we're still doing fine." Zeke kept his sigh to himself and sat on the sofa, crossing his ankle over his knee. "I'll dig through the numbers myself tonight."

"No need. You're right." He pushed to his feet and downed the remaining whiskey in his glass. "I probably added things up wrong. You know your Aunt Sybil. I have to keep her in diamonds and furs."

Right. His aunt wouldn't dare ask for anything. While his uncle did shower his wife with gifts, Zeke suspected they were more for appearance than out of love. Poor Sybil scurried to do his bidding like a timid field mouse.

Zeke would still go over the numbers. His uncle had changed tactics too quickly. Something wasn't right.

Chapter Four

A new snowfall greeted Shea the next morning. All traces of Zeke's footprints were covered. The only evidence he'd been there was the stack of freshly cut firewood. Surprisingly, she'd enjoyed their short visit drinking coffee.

He'd hinted a few times in regard to the papers on the table, but he hadn't pressed the issue or taken a peek at them. Maybe he really was one of the good guys.

Shea wiggled her feet into slippers to ward off the bitter chill in her bedroom. Why didn't the house have central heating? She wasn't used to having to keep a fire burning all night.

After several attempts to grasp a match with frozen fingers, she got a fire burning. The small place would heat up quickly. Coffee would help. The thought of a shower that morning made her decide to purchase some space heaters after work.

Minutes later, a cup of hot coffee in her hand, she stood at the window nearest the fireplace and sipped her drink while watching the snow fall.

She'd stayed up late the night before poring over the files from her father's murder. Nothing new had been dug up. Still, there was no doubt Buford was responsible.

He'd been at that bar, had words with her father, even thrown a punch from what witnesses said. Who else would have had a motive to lie in wait while her father arrived at a domestic dispute and shot him sniper-style? She'd find the evidence needed and make sure her dad had justice.

When she'd finished her coffee, Shea set the cup in the sink, collected her clothes from the bedroom, and dressed in front of the fire. She retrieved her gun and badge from her nightstand, shrugged into a thick coat, and stepped into a winter wonderland.

She turned on her truck's heater then scraped snow from her windshield with a spatula she'd brought with her. As the snow moved away, a sheet of paper fluttered under the windshield wiper.

Frowning, Shea bent close to read the smeared print. *"Leave town without asking questions."*

She grinned. Yep, she was definitely in the right place. No one could frighten her from her mission. Shea wadded the paper into a ball and threw it on the passenger-side floor. With a good glance around the area, she climbed into her truck and drove to work.

"You look pretty pleased with yourself." Graham glanced up from his computer.

"Slept good." She smiled, hung her coat on a hook, and sat at her desk. "Anything going on today?"

"Not yet. The snow is keeping the troublemakers inside."

Good. That would give her some time to dig around online. The computers in the department allowed her access to things hers at home didn't.

She compiled a list of names of men and women who had worked with Buford when he was mayor.

Graham wouldn't know much about the people since he'd arrived only a few months before she did. "Who around these parts knows everything about everyone? Every small town has a person like that, don't they?"

"Sure. Ole Wilbur would know. He hangs out at the diner every day for every meal. Then, there's June Mayfield, but she rarely leaves her house. Why?"

"It's always useful for local law enforcement to know who to question when something happens."

A man and woman in deputy uniforms entered the room.

"About time the two of you decided to get off vacation and back to work." Graham stood. "Deputy Johnson, Deputy Young, meet our new deputy, Shea Sydney."

They both nodded and took their seats. "Slow day?" Johnson asked.

"Yep."

"I'm surprised a town the size of Misty Hollow needs four deputies." Shea glanced from one face to the other.

"With all the recent crime over the last year or so," Young said, "we need the extra help. We've gone a few months now without too much trouble." She didn't look as if she liked the slower pace. "Welcome to the small town with lots of secrets."

"Thanks." Shea planned on adding her own secret to shake things up. She bit her tongue to keep from blurting out about the warning note. "I'm sure I'll like it here."

"Good morning." Sheriff Westbrook stood in the doorway. "I see you've all met. The snow is clearing, and there seems to be an upset at that biker bar just outside of town. Shea and Graham, why don't the two of you take that? Gives Shea a chance to soak up some local color. Johnson and Young, there's an accident on the interstate and a couple of very angry drivers."

"Come on." Graham motioned to Shea. "When we're done there, we'll pop into Lucy's Diner for lunch, and I'll introduce you to Wilbur."

Sounded like a plan. Shea put her coat back on and followed him to a squad car.

Motorcycles lined the front of a wood-shingled building. A couple of men wearing leather vests squared off in the parking lot, a circle forming around them. One of the fighters sported a bloody lip.

"A bit insane to fight during a snowfall." Shea shoved her door open then marched toward the two men. "Break it up, gentlemen." She donned her sternest cop expression and flashed her badge. "Deputy Sydney. Time for you two to go home."

The largest of the two whipped around to face her. "Well, ain't you a purty thang? Move on, sweetheart. My brother and I have some discussing to do."

His brother? "Take your sibling rivalry somewhere else, sir." She moved the edge of her coat aside to reveal her weapon.

"You going to shoot me?" He laughed, glancing around the circle. "Look at that, boys. The little girl wants to play rough."

"Enough, Dewayne." Graham moved closer to Shea. "Go home and sleep it off. Looks like you've been here all night."

"We have. I'm getting married. This is my bachelor party."

"Then why the fight?" Shea tilted her head.

"Because my little brother wouldn't buy me another drink."

~

So, the new deputy wasn't shy. He slowed as he passed the biker bar, surprised to see her. Since she and O'Connor wore plain clothes, he'd almost missed her. How had she liked his little warning? Somehow, he doubted she'd heed it. The woman was tougher than most. Maybe he'd have to be a little more direct.

If she dug deep enough, she'd find things best left hidden. Her father had been dead for ten years. Why bring it all back up?

He shook his head and increased his speed. A man had business to do. He couldn't spy on Deputy Sydney all the time.

He drummed his fingers on the steering wheel as he tried to devise a way to meet her. Maybe become friends, someone she'd confide in. Who knew—maybe she was a woman who liked older men. He grinned.

Shouldn't be that hard. He glanced in the rearview mirror. His looks, charm, and money hadn't gone south yet.

~

Zeke glanced up as Shea and Graham entered the diner. Graham introduced her to Wilbur, whose rugged, wrinkled face lit up.

"About time we got another looker in this town," the old man said. "What kind of trouble did you bring with you? Every time a pretty girl arrives, trouble shows up."

Zeke shook his head. If only Wilbur knew what chaos the new deputy could stir up. He called out a greeting and invited them to his booth. "I'm just about to order."

"Great." Graham waved Shea onto the bench with Zeke and slid in opposite them. "Shea wanted to meet Wilbur."

"The man knows everyone." Zeke smiled and glanced at the laminated menu in his hand although he always ordered the same thing the few times he actually came to the diner. Chicken fried steak with potatoes and gravy. He closed his menu.

A subtle gardenia fragrance drifted from Shea. He hadn't pictured her as a flowery type of woman, but he liked it.

"You ought to have your partner bake some cookies," he said. "The best I've had."

"What's up with that?" Graham arched a brow. "Can't spare any for me, but you gave some to this rich yahoo?"

"He just showed up at my doorstep."

"Were you warm enough last night?" Zeke faced her.

"Froze my tush off, truth be told. I let the fire go out. On the way home, I'm buying space heaters after work today."

"My car is in the shop for maintenance. Would it be too much trouble if I bummed a ride off you? I can stay here in the diner until you pick me up. There are enough things to keep me occupied." Zeke made a gesture toward his laptop on the other side of the table.

"Sure, if you don't mind stopping at the hardware store."

"Don't mind a bit. I'll have the chicken fried steak meal." He handed his menu to the server.

"Chef salad, large, dressing on the side, and a diet soda." Shea handed hers over.

Graham ordered a burger with everything. "Looks like Shea is the only sensible eater here."

Which definitely looked good on her. Zeke ducked his head and smiled.

The three chatted about nothing in particular, pointing out residents of interest to Shea as people came and went. Once lunch was over, the two deputies returned to work, and Zeke spent the rest of the afternoon poring over the vineyard's books. By the time Shea returned, he still hadn't figured out what his uncle was hiding from him.

He closed the laptop, paid for the copious amount of cups of coffee he'd had, and followed her into the snow. "Looks like it'll storm tonight."

"Here's hoping I can purchase some heaters. At least three. One each for the bedroom, the bathroom, and the front room. I'm no good with fireplaces." She slid into the driver's seat.

Zeke climbed in, setting his laptop on the floor between his feet. "I appreciate the ride."

"You've helped me plenty of times." She backed from the parking spot and drove down Main Street to the hardware store.

Zeke's favorite place. His spirit lifted at the sight of tools, building supplies, chicken coops, and more. The place smelled of tires and animal feed. Maybe it was time to purchase some chickens. He'd always wanted to. He eyed a coop. In the spring, he would.

Shea purchased her three porcelain heaters and carried them to the counter. "No more freezing."

He laughed. "If you'd kept the fire going, you wouldn't have frozen. You'd have been tossing off the blankets."

"Then these will help me regulate the temperature better." She paid for her purchases and carried them to her truck and into the backseat.

The snow fell harder, keeping its promise of an upcoming storm. "Will you be all right alone? We could lose power."

"If we do, then I'll resort to the fire for warmth and sleep on the sofa. Relax, Zeke. I'm not your problem."

"We're neighbors. That's what neighbors do." He bent to retrieve his laptop from the floor as she pulled in front of his house.

A wadded-up piece of paper rolled toward him as she stopped. He picked it up and started to hand it to her.

The shocked, worried look on her face gave him pause. Without asking, he unrolled the paper and read the warning there. Now, he definitely didn't want her home alone during a storm. "Come to my place. Stay here. I can keep you safe."

"I'll be perfectly fine." She snatched the warning from his fingers. "Goodnight, Zeke."

He climbed out of the truck knowing it wouldn't be a good night. He'd be awake, staring out the upstairs window, watching her house.

Chapter Five

The snow was still falling the next morning. Since crime didn't sleep, Shea had to go to work. She turned off the space heaters and stepped reluctantly into the bitter cold.

Zeke hunkered down next to her truck, his head and shoulders covered with snow. He glanced up and grinned. "I figured you didn't know how to put on snow chains, so I did it for you."

"Thank you." He really was a genuinely nice guy.

He pushed to his feet and brushed the snow from his coat and hat. "You're all set. I've some deliveries to make, but call me if you get stuck."

"Wouldn't it be better to call a tow truck?" She cocked her head.

"Ah. Right." He chuckled and climbed into his truck. With a wave, he backed from her drive and drove away.

Perhaps Shea wasn't used to country or mountain people. Other than Buford being surly when they met or the guy at the biker bar, everyone smiled and waved whether they knew her or not.

She shrugged and climbed into her truck, cranking the heater up and shivering until the cold dispelled. She'd forgotten to scrape her window. With a groan, she got back out, cleared the window, and slid into a now warming truck. Getting used to friendly people wasn't the only thing she needed to do. She also had to learn how to deal with the cold and snow.

Halfway to town, she spotted two vehicles on the side of the road and slowed to see whether they needed aid. Her eyes widened to see a red-faced Zeke glaring at a man who shouted mere inches from his face. She stopped and rolled down her window. A slap of icy wind greeted her.

Other cars slowed to see what was going on. Shea waved them forward.

"Everyone all right here?" She glanced at Zeke.

"We're fine, Deputy."

He didn't look fine. If he clenched his jaw any tighter, he'd crack a tooth. "What's going on here?"

"This guy—" the other man jabbed a finger into Zeke's chest. "shorted me on an order."

"You're mistaken," Zeke growled.

Shea slipped out of her truck, leaving the engine running. Things were escalating between the two men faster than she liked.

"Sir, please do not have physical contact with Mr. Matchett. I'm sure if the two of you discuss the matter in a calm—"

"I'm done discussing. Mark my words, Matchett. You'll get yours one day. Crooked people don't go unpunished."

"We'll see, Mr. Hudson. We'll see." Sparing Shea the barest of glances, he marched to his truck. He fishtailed onto the road and sped off. The other man sped in the opposite direction. Well, it appeared Zeke might be human after all.

She returned to an overly warm truck and finished the drive into town. "Sorry I'm late." She hung her coat on a hook in the bullpen.

"Nothing happening anyway. With those roads—" Graham shook his head, "most people are driving a lot slower."

"Do you know a Mr. Hudson?"

"He's the owner of the bar we went to. Why?"

She told him of the encounter on the highway. "Seems a bit of a hothead."

"I've heard the man has a temper." Graham returned to his computer.

Shea's desk phone rang. She didn't have a chance to say hello before Doris, the receptionist, blurted out there'd been a murder at the Chug a Mug aka biker bar.

"Murder?" Shea hung up the phone and grabbed her coat. "Biker bar. I'll drive." She flashed a grin and snatched the keys from her hand.

Graham's throaty laugh followed her into the hallway.

Fifteen minutes later, they entered the bar. A pale-faced bartender motioned to the back. Video cameras were mounted in every corner.

Shea's steps faltered as her gaze landed on Zeke. He sat at a table, hands cuffed in front of him while Deputy Johnson stood guard.

"In here." Deputy Young motioned her forward. "Owner found stabbed with one of the knives at the bar. The bartender found Mr. Matchett standing over him. There were several broken bottles of the wine Matchett makes."

"You're considering him a person of interest?" The

fact that Zeke and the victim had been in an altercation earlier that day wouldn't help his case.

Shea and Graham stepped into a small room full of wine cases and boxes of liquor. On the floor lay Mr. Hudson, a white handled knife in his chest. Around his head were multiple shattered bottles. At the opposite end of the room was a door.

Shea stepped around the corpse and turned the door handle. It opened easily at her touch. Had the killer come through the back or…she glanced in the direction where Zeke sat. Had he come under the pretense of making a delivery? Some seemingly "nice guys" had turned out to be the best serial killers in the past.

No. Her gut told her Zeke wouldn't be capable of this.

"What are you thinking?" Young studied her face.

"That the killer came through the back door."

"Matchett entered through the front."

"He didn't kill this man. It would be a foolish thing to do—waltz through the front door and brazenly kill someone only to stick around and be found out."

"A rage killing. Unprecedented."

She shook her head. "I'll stake my badge on the fact that Zeke Matchett isn't capable of murder." Shea prayed she wouldn't come to regret those words.

~

Zeke stood when Shea emerged from the back room only to have the large deputy put a hand on his shoulder and shove him back onto the seat. "I want to speak with Deputy Sydney. In private."

"It's all right." Shea gave the man a nod. "Stand over by the bar, please." She sat across from Zeke. "You okay?"

"I didn't kill him."

"I seriously doubt that you did. Mind telling me what happened?" She set a large paper tablet on the table and pulled an ink pen from her coat jacket. At his questioning look, she said, "Just taking notes."

"I made my delivery as planned. Knew that Hudson wanted the bottles taken directly into the stockroom, so that's where I headed. I found him on the floor. The bartender came up behind me and started yelling that I'd killed him. He wouldn't listen to reason. I was upfront about arguing with Hudson earlier today. That's when the deputy cuffed me."

"You didn't see anyone else?"

"No. So, the bartender called the sheriff's department and held a gun on me until they...you arrived."

Her eyes narrowed. "Would you have run?"

"Of course not." He tried crossing his arms, sighed, and set his cuffed hands back on the table.

"Don't worry. You've no blood on you. Standing over the corpse isn't a crime." She moved to the other two deputies.

Zeke did his best to read their lips and failed. Surely, they'd see the holes in the story they tried to put together. He hadn't been in the bar long enough to have done the deed.

Shea pointed to one of the cameras. "Are those working and have a time stamp on them?"

The bartender nodded. "I'll show you."

Some of the tension left Zeke's shoulders. The cameras would be his alibi.

Half an hour later, Shea uncuffed him. "You didn't have enough time to kill Mr. Hudson. The bartender arrived mere seconds after you did. All you need to do now is come to the station to fill out a statement." She smiled and stepped back.

"Thank you." He rubbed his wrists. "Good thing the camera doesn't lie."

Shea returned to the crime scene, leaving Zeke to wonder whether he could leave the bar or not. Were they finished with him? He pointed to the door. Shea nodded. Relief flooded through him, catching his breath. The closer he got to outside, the easier he could breathe. The fear of going to jail for a horrid crime he didn't commit had rattled him good.

In his truck, he sat with his head down and his hands on the steering wheel. Zeke wasn't naïve, but he'd never seen anything other than a dead animal during hunting season. Never had he seen anyone murdered.

A tapping on his window drew his attention. He looked over to see a worried Shea and rolled his window down.

"You okay?"

"Yeah, just a little shook up. I don't know how law enforcement gets used to seeing that."

"We don't." A shadow crossed her features. "We've learned to shove it aside and do the job." She put a hand on the truck door. "I'll follow you to the office, get you a cup of really bad coffee, and take your statement."

"Worried about me, Deputy?" His mouth twitched.

"Seeing your first murder victim shakes a person up." She smiled and headed for her truck.

At the sheriff's office, he waited for her to pull into a spot before exiting his truck. "I'm grateful you believed me."

"You're sickeningly sweet, Zeke. Unless you're a

very good actor, you couldn't have killed that man."

"Sickeningly sweet?" That's how she thought of him?

"No offense, but I've never met anyone like you." He could say the same about her. Zeke reached around her to open the door to the building. "I'm courteous, not sweet. Women are sweet." Unless they're Shea. She had more flavor than any sugary treat.

She motioned toward the chair across from her desk in a bullpen that had room for maybe one more desk if a good game of Tetris was played with the furniture. "I'll bring that coffee. Fill this out, please." She handed him a clipboard with a few pages on it.

A few minutes later, forms filled out, Zeke took a sip of a cup of hot, very strong, black coffee. "Who makes this?" He frowned.

"Doris. Her feelings get hurt if anyone says anything or makes the coffee themselves. We suffer through it for her."

"I'm not sure I can." He set it on the desk. "Am I free to go?"

"Yes." She picked up the cup, took a sip, and grimaced.

Seeing how she'd drink the bad cup of java to spare someone's feelings made him want to kiss her. Just like that, out of the blue, plant one on her. Instead, he smiled and left the room before he did something that would get him handcuffed again.

Back at his house, he checked emails, logged in the deliveries he'd made that day, and made himself a good cup of coffee then settled down to continue poring over the books. Again, something seemed off, but he couldn't pinpoint the…he noticed the name Chug a Mug, except in his uncle's handwriting. The spelling was similar but not the same as Zeke's Chugg a Mugg.

He straightened in his chair. A simply misspelling, or something else? Zeke flipped through the book. Sometimes, it was written Chug a Mug and others with two g's. He would not have made that mistake. His uncle had inserted a fake account. Since Zeke could keep the logs almost on autopilot, he skimmed right over the misspelling.

Was Buford embezzling from the vineyard?

~

Stupid wine maker. Served him right for being a suspect. The instant the door handle had turned, he'd run out the back. Hudson had barely taken his last breath before Matchett strolled in. Too close of a call for comfort.

He turned on the Sawzall he carried in his trunk and sawed the head off the deer he'd struck. No sense letting any meat go to waste. Not when it fell right in front of him. He eyed the dented bumper. The vehicle would run just fine, and the local garage was used to fixing the damage hitting a deer caused.

After preparing the deer, he tossed the edible parts and the head into his trunk, leaving the entrails for the buzzards and other critters. He had a great plan for the head and wished he could stick around to see the aftermath.

One way or another, he'd convince the pretty new deputy to leave town.

Chapter Six

Thankfully, Shea woke to a winter wonderland as far as the eye could see. A bright blue sky cast diamonds on the ground's surface. Tree branches bowed under white blankets. She smiled and sipped her coffee while she feasted on the view outside her rented home. Nothing could dispel her good mood, not even the fact she still didn't have proof that Buford killed her father.

She'd made a list of people to question on her day off. With Hudson's murder, she didn't have a lot of time to investigate a cold case. Setting her empty cup in the sink, she readied herself for the day.

Half an hour later, she opened her front door and tripped over something in her path. Her arms windmilled as she tried to keep her balance. Instead, she plunged off the porch and fell face first into the snow.

She rolled onto her back to catch her breath then made a snow angel with her arms and legs, struggling to a sitting position. When she could breathe easily again, she pushed to her feet and went to see what she'd tripped over.

A deer's head stared at her with lifeless eyes. Since it was freezing outside, no flies buzzed around it. Shea pulled her cell phone from her coat pocket and snapped a photo. Someone wanted her gone. She smiled. It would take a lot more than a dead deer to scare her away.

At work, she showed Graham the photo. "Looks like someone is welcoming me to Misty Hollow."

"Why would anyone threaten you? You haven't been here long enough to anger anyone."

She shrugged. "I'm stepping on someone's toes." No need to tell him why she really came to town. "I wanted to head back to the bar and do some digging for clues behind the building, but this snow would have covered everything up."

"Hopefully the new owner will install cameras in back."

"Hopefully there won't be another murder."

"Yeah, that too."

The rest of the morning she spent reading everything she could find online about Buford. When she couldn't find anything new, she invited Graham to lunch.

"Not this time. I've some errands to run. Thanks, though." He grabbed his coat.

"No problem." This was even better. She wanted to ask Wilbur some questions without Graham wondering about her interest in Buford. The fewer people who knew about her asking about the man, the better. "Stay safe. The roads are slick."

Shea needed to do her actual job, too, and find out whether anyone near the bar might have seen someone around back. The bartender had just arrived and hadn't seen anything. Then, there was the list she'd made of people who used to work for or with Buford. She'd be asking a lot of questions. Someone already wanted her to stop, but she was only getting started.

As usual, the diner was full. Shea grabbed a stool at the counter before someone got there first. She ordered the day's special, a cheesy potato soup, and settled in.

"How do you like our fair town?" Wilbur asked.

"Well enough." She smiled, grateful he'd struck up the conversation first. "There are a lot of colorful characters."

He laughed. "Me being one of them."

"And Buford Matchett. He doesn't exactly exude southern charm."

"Oh, he had plenty of that when he was the mayor. Sweet words flowed from his lips like a waterfall after a rainstorm. Didn't take long for his true colors to show through though."

"Oh?" She thanked the waitress for bringing her soup.

"His wife, Sybil, couldn't always hide the bruises. My dear late wife was a nurse over in Langley. Said the mayor's wife came in more times than a woman should for something broken."

"A wife beater?"

He nodded. "That's why he wasn't reelected. Lives in a big ole log cabin high on the mountain where he can look over the valley as if he's the lord of Misty Hollow. Folks around here don't much care for the man, and his missus rarely leaves their house."

Mrs. Matchett could be a well of information. "Does she receive visitors?"

"Don't know. I've never tried. You might want to ask June Mayfield. Until the murder of her best friend, she visited once in a while to check on Sybil. June lives over on Oak Street. Big Victorian on the corner. Can't miss it."

"Thank you very much." She dug into her lunch while Wilbur rattled on about other town citizens. People who didn't have much to do with Buford. Her ears perked up at the mention of a man named David Real. "He was Buford's right hand when he was mayor, right?"

"That's right. You've done your homework." Wilbur beamed.

"Where would I find Mr. Real?"

"He lives over by the lake. Never been to his house before, but someone out that way can point you in the right direction."

"You, sir, should have been in law enforcement."

He laughed. "Folks wouldn't tell me much if I was. You know anything about who killed Hudson?"

"Not yet. If you hear anything, give me a call." She slapped enough cash on the counter to pay for her soup and a tip before rushing out the door, colliding with Zeke.

~

"Whoa." Zeke put his hands on Shea's shoulders to steady her. "Where are you headed in such a hurry?"

"Deputy business." She stepped back. Her eyes widened at the sight of a photograph on the ground.

Zeke snatched it before she could. "What's this?" He stared at the photo of a deer head.

"A present left on my porch. Give it back. It's evidence." She grabbed it from his fingers.

"First the note, now this. What is going on?" Someone really had their eye on Shea and not in a good way.

"I aim to find out. Excuse me." She brushed past him then stopped and turned. "Did you see anyone at the bar when you discovered the body other than the bartender? Were there any cars in the parking lot? Motorcycles?"

He blinked a few times trying to remember. "I didn't see one, but I do recall the screech of tires out back when I stood over Hudson's body."

She nodded. "Further proof the killer most likely must have come through the back. If you remember anything else, let me know." She continued to her truck, jumping inside too fast for Zeke to protest further.

He didn't like it one bit that someone had left the head on her porch. Worry filled him as he entered the diner and took a seat at the counter.

"The new deputy just left that seat," Wilbur said. "Nice gal. We had a good conversation. She's a bit nosy about your uncle, though."

"Really?"

"Asked a lot of questions about his time as mayor, Sybil, where he lived…" He slurped his black coffee. "Seems more interested in Buford than in who killed Hudson."

Zeke ordered a Philly cheesesteak sandwich. "Maybe she's just trying to find out about the town."

"Said she was interested in colorful characters. Nice but a bit strange, if you ask me."

Buford would blow a gasket if he found out Shea was asking about him. Since the failed reelection, he rarely came down off the mountain anymore unless it was to harass Zeke and "look" at the books. Find out how much he could pilfer was more like it.

"I think she's going to be visiting June Mayfield and David Real."

"Why?" Zeke faced him.

"June knows Sybil, and David used to work for

him." Wilbur looked at him as if he were going senile. "Why else?"

Zeke heaved a sigh. Once she questioned David, then his uncle would know for sure she was checking on him. The two men were still as close as twins in the womb. He needed to find a way to stop her before something bad really happened to her.

Would his uncle have put the deer head on her porch? No, but he could have paid someone else to do it. There were still plenty of people willing to do Buford's bidding. If—and it was a big if—Buford actually had anything to do with what was going on with Shea. But if not him, then who?

He scarfed down his food and drove to the sheriff's office only to discover Shea wasn't there. Next, he drove to June's. Shea's white truck sat out front. He couldn't very well go knock on the door of a woman he'd never officially met.

Shea stepped off the porch. June must not be home.

When she saw him idling in front of the house next door, she marched his way. Her expressionless face, her cop face, could have been chiseled from stone. She rapped on his window.

He rolled it down. "Hey."

"Are you following me?"

"Yes."

That knocked a little of the stoniness from her features. She blinked in confusion. "Why?"

"I need to talk to you. We can do it here, or I can follow you to your office." He knew her answer before she gave one. The office would have people close enough to hear her business.

She climbed into his truck. "Here is fine."

He rolled his head on his shoulders wondering what would be the best way to request that she stop asking questions. "Why the interest in my uncle?"

"It pertains to a case."

"The one on your kitchen table?"

She frowned. "Possibly."

"Look. Buford is not a man to mess with. He has friends in high places. My uncle could get you fired."

"I don't take the sheriff to be a man who would hold his hand out to a man like Buford."

She was right. Sheriff Westbrook would never take dirty money. Time to switch tactics. "He doesn't treat women right. Buford has no qualms about hitting a woman. He'll make your life a living hell, Shea. Unless you have absolute proof he's the man you're looking for, I'm asking you to back off."

"Won't happen." She crossed her arms.

"What do you think he did?"

"Killed my father. Shot him like a sniper." Her eyes glistened. "I'm going to prove he did, Zeke. And I don't need your approval." She met his eyes. "Do not tell your uncle."

"I won't, but someone else will." He rubbed his hands briskly down his face. How could he convince her to see reason? "My uncle is many things, but he wouldn't have jeopardized his career for murder."

"Not even if he'd been drinking? My father and Buford had an altercation shortly before his murder. Dad showed up to a domestic dispute and was shot. That dispute was at your uncle's house, who just happened to be missing by the time my father showed up. Coincidence? I don't think so." The imploring look in her eyes was almost his undoing. "Can't you see him killing someone?"

Could Buford have committed murder? Murder was a far cry from embezzlement and extortion, but there was the abuse. Zeke's heart sank. Yes, he could see his uncle ending someone's life in a fit of rage.

How in the world could he keep Shea out of the clutches of Buford?

Chapter Seven

The melting of the snow left Shea and Graham behind the Chug a Mug with slim hopes of finding anything. Mud covered every surface not made of concrete or asphalt. Since the investigation was ongoing, the bar had not reopened.

"Who would want to kill Hudson?" Shea studied the tire tracks preserved in the mud by the freeze. "Tell me someone took a mold of this."

"They did. The garage owner is comparing them to his records. Maybe we'll get lucky."

Here's hoping. Shea needed luck in this case and the cold case. She'd really thought by coming to Misty Hollow she'd have found the proof she needed by now. Her conversation with Wilbur had only raised more questions.

Tomorrow was her day off. Being new to the department, she had Thursday and Friday off instead of weekends like the other deputies. She'd spend both those days pounding the pavement in search of answers. "What kind of man is David Real?"

"Haven't met him." Graham studied the area around the back door. "I don't think we're going to find anything more here. Without an eyewitness, Hudson's murderer may never be found."

Shea refused to have another cold case on her hands. "I read the sheriff's department has a high success rate."

"It does, but usually several people have to die first. Then the bad guy messes up, and bam, we got 'em."

That didn't say much for the department.

"It'll be better now. The department only had two deputies in the past, plus the sheriff, and resources were stretched thin."

They questioned the bartender again, a server, and still had nothing. No one other than Zeke and the bartender were on the cameras. No footprints outside. The tire tracks probably belonged to the owner. Shea wasn't holding onto much hope.

After lunch, she headed out on her own and returned to June Mayfield's house. A tiny woman who looked as if a stiff wind could blow her away answered the door.

"I'm the new deputy, Shea Sydney. Would you be able to answer some questions for me?"

"I'm not sure I can, but I'm willing to try. Come on in. I've fresh cookies and coffee."

Somehow, Shea suspected she always had cookies ready for unexpected company. "Thank you." She shed her coat and hung it on a coat tree. "I'm trying to get a feel for Misty Hollow, and Wilbur at the diner told me you knew everything about everyone."

June smiled, her face dissolving into wrinkles. "I pride myself on the fact I'm a nosy woman, but I've never had anyone come by to get a feel for the folks of this town." She motioned to a chair at the table. "Why don't you tell me why you're really here?"

There was no getting past this woman. Shea should have known by the intelligent glint in her eyes. She chuckled and took a chocolate-chip cookie. "I was told you are friends with Sybil Matchett."

"Yes, although I haven't seen her outside of church in over a year."

Shea hadn't expected to hear that Buford and his wife attended church. Wife beaters didn't seem the type.

"Is this about Sybil?"

"More about Buford." How much should she tell? "You wouldn't happen to know where he was on August 18th, ten years ago, would you?"

"My old brain will take a minute on that one. Stay right there." She bustled down the hall, returning a few minutes later with an armful of books. "I keep a daily diary and save them for my grandson to read through one day. They'll probably bore him to tears, but I can't bear to throw them away at the end of each year. I might not be able to tell you where Buford was that day, but if there was an event, he will have been there. That day was during his mayor days."

She opened the book of that year and flipped to August. "Aha. He would have been at the revival. It would've looked bad for him if he wasn't there."

"Are you sure?"

"Absolutely. Buford was all about appearances back then. In public, at least."

That threw Shea's theory that Buford killed her father out the window. Maybe June was mistaken.

"I know what. Hold on." She left again, returning with a newspaper. "There." She tapped the front page of the *Misty Hollow Gazette.*

A black and white photo depicting a group of men, one of them Buford, covered the front page. "He was a deacon?"

"Yep. There's your proof that he was at the revival." She pointed to the date.

Shea was chasing the wrong man. Her throat burned as she fought back tears. She'd been so certain Buford had killed her father that she no longer knew what to do next. He could have hired someone. Buford could have attended the revival to have an alibi while still being behind the murder. "Thank you, June. You've been a big help."

"Whatever you're looking for, I hope you find it, Deputy. Stop by anytime. I'm always glad for the company."

Shea nodded and stood. "You keep on being nosy, Ms. Mayfield. Folks like you are an asset to the department."

Shea grabbed her coat and stepped outside, freezing in place at the sight of Zeke's truck. Why couldn't the man get it through his head to stop stalking her? She squared her shoulders and marched toward him.

"What are you doing here?" She fought to tamp down her anger.

"I saw your truck and knew you were still asking questions about my uncle. I've also told you how dangerous that is, so I'm here to make sure nothing happens to you."

~

So, the deer head hadn't done anything to keep the deputy from sticking her nose where it didn't belong. He drove by the old woman's house, craning his neck to see the deputy march to Matchett's vehicle.

He'd really thought that casting the shadow on Zeke for killing Hudson would have kept the deputy's focus on solving that crime instead of one that had happened ten years ago. He slammed his palm on the steering wheel and turned a corner onto another street.

What he needed was a better plan. He needed to up the stakes, but this woman wouldn't scare easily. Maybe he should leave things alone. No one had solved the case in all this time. All the trails would've grown cold. Yes, he most likely worried over nothing and should step aside.

More threats and warnings would only make her dig deeper.

The weight he'd been carrying slid from his shoulders. He'd worked himself into a frenzy for nothing. Killed Hudson for no reason, not that it bothered him that much. He'd never liked the self-righteous man, and after killing Detective Sydney, what was one more?

~

"It's all moot anyway. There's no way your uncle could have pulled the trigger on the gun that killed my father." Shea sighed. "He'd been in town at a revival."

Zeke nodded. "He never missed one while mayor."

"So, you worried for nothing." She turned to leave, shuffling toward her truck.

"Stop, Shea." He shoved his door open and followed. "That doesn't explain the deer head or the written warning. Whoever is leaving those, whether it's Buford or not, is still out there."

She faced him. "What can you do about that?"

"I want you to come stay at the vineyard with me. The property has all the latest security—"

"Absolutely not. I'm law enforcement, and I'm perfectly capable of taking care of myself."

Why wouldn't she listen to him? "Buford comes by a few times a week. You'd be right there when he does."

The light in her eyes told him he might be on to something. "He goes over the books, has a drink, we talk a bit, then he leaves. You could study him, determine whether or not he could actually have something to do with your father's death. Plus—" he went for the zinger, "I go to his place every Sunday after church." He grinned. "You'd see his house, meet his wife…"

"Fine." She shook her head. "You're a horrible man, Zeke Matchett." A smile teased at her lips. "Dangling a carrot like that in front of my face, knowing I couldn't refuse. I'll pack up some things and be over before dark."

"I'll fix supper." Pleased with himself, he headed home to prepare the guest room. Buford would have a fit when he found out the deputy resided under Zeke's roof. Not only did Zeke want to give Shea the opportunity to observe his uncle, but he hoped his uncle would stop skimming money from the books with a deputy under the same roof. That would give Zeke time to come up with a plan to confront Buford and take his share of the vineyard.

He pulled his truck into the garage then hurried in the house to put fresh sheets on the guest bed down the hall from Zeke's room. Then, he made sure the bathroom was fully stocked before placing an order for a delivery of groceries from the local market. When he stayed there alone, he kept groceries to a bare minimum, choosing to pick something up on his way home.

"What has you all worked up?" Buford asked when Zeke returned to the living room.

"Deputy Sydney will be staying here for a few days." He waited for the explosion.

"What the hell for?" His uncle lunged to his feet, spilling a bit of the whiskey in the glass he held. "We don't want her here. Are you crazy?"

Zeke frowned. "What's the problem? We aren't doing anything illegal, and she needs a warm place to spend a few days. There's no heat in her rental other than a fireplace and some space heaters."

"So? Buy her more heaters. I won't have her here."

"It's my house. Buck left it to me not you." Zeke sat and propped an ankle over his knee. "Which means, I can have anyone stay here I want."

"You're going to regret this, mark my words." He slammed the glass on the mantel and stormed from the house.

Zeke laughed. His uncle had taken the news as expected. The bad thing was, he'd be by more often in order to keep an eye on the deputy. Which meant Zeke's peaceful evenings would be few and far between.

By the time Shea arrived a little after six, Zeke was flipping the steaks and vegetables on the grill.

"You're crazy cooking outside in this cold. There's another storm predicted tonight." Shea set a large duffel bag on the kitchen table.

"It's never too cold to grill. Let me show you to your room." He led her down the hall. "Oh, and my uncle isn't pleased you're staying here."

She arched a brow. "You told him?"

"Buford stopped by. He'll be rude, but I'm sure you can handle him. Supper will be ready in fifteen minutes. Make yourself comfortable."

"What can I help with?"

"Tonight? Nothing. I'll put you to work tomorrow." He smiled and headed back outside to turn the steaks.

As he did, he wondered whether he could elicit Shea's help with his uncle's embezzling without making it an official case for the department. Something for her to help with off the books, so to speak. It wouldn't hurt to ask. Then, she'd have a legitimate reason to dig into Buford's life. If it turned out he murdered her father, they'd have him on two accounts.

The man would finally be out of the picture. Sybil would no longer feel the brunt of his fists, and Zeke could run the vineyard as he saw fit.

It would be best for everyone.

Chapter Eight

Shea woke disoriented the next morning. She blinked until the grey light of another wintery morning came in clearer. Her hands rubbed the fabric of the thick quilt. Right. Zeke's house.

Her hands stretched across the king-sized bed. A canopy draped overhead. She turned her head and watched as fat, lazy snowflakes drifted past the window. Zeke was right. His sprawling home was definitely warmer than her rental. Still, she wouldn't allow herself to grow too complacent. Once she knew who killed her father, Shea would leave Misty Hollow.

The aroma of brewed coffee lured her from bed. She padded to the kitchen in baggy cotton pants and an oversized tee shirt.

Zeke turned, a smile on his face. "Somehow, I knew you didn't sleep in anything girly." He handed her a mug.

Too early for banter. She mumbled a thanks and poured vanilla-flavored creamer in her coffee before sitting at the table.

"Not a morning person. Got it." Zeke turned back to the stove. "I hope pancakes are okay. Today seems a fitting day for a stack with maple syrup."

Shea preferred butter and powdered sugar but

wouldn't be picky. The man simply did his thing. Be nice, Shea. What would he be like if someone really riled him up? She might pay to see that. Low embers burned the hottest. At least that's how she thought the saying went.

Today being her day off, she itched to bake something. Baking helped clear her mind of clutter and think more clearly. She glanced out the window at the snowbanks. Only a crazy person or one who had to get to work would go out on a day like today.

Zeke set a plate with three pancakes in front of her. "What are your plans for your day off?"

"I'm not sure. I'd like to buy ingredients to make a cake, but going out in that isn't very appealing." She peered outside then eyed the syrup.

"Would you like something else?"

"Do you have powdered sugar and butter?"

"Sure do." He opened a pantry the size of most people's bathrooms and pulled out a bag of powdered sugar. From the fridge, he grabbed a butter dish, setting both in front of her. "I'm pretty sure I have anything you need, but if not, we can have it delivered."

"You keep your pantry stocked?"

"With sweets I do." He laughed. "As for food that's good for you, not so much. I usually eat on the run or bring home takeout."

She eyed his well-kept physique. "Why aren't you fat?" Or married? A person would think Zeke to be the most eligible bachelor of the town, if not the whole state. She bit her tongue to keep from asking.

His laugh deepened. "I stay very busy."

The pancakes were light and fluffy. Better than any she'd had in a restaurant. She ate half and pushed her plate to the side. "Is Buford coming today?"

"Since you're here, I'm going to say yes. He won't miss the chance to try to intimidate you."

"That won't be easy."

He studied her face for a minute. "It probably won't be. That means he'll try harder the next time."

Let him. Shea considered herself up for the challenge.

After she helped Zeke clean up the breakfast dishes, she took a peek in his pantry. Plenty of ingredients to bake a cake and hardly anything of substance. The man really needed to start eating better. She rubbed her hands together and pulled out the items she needed before heading to take a shower.

Clean and dressed in yoga pants and a large sweatshirt, she returned to the kitchen, surprised to see Zeke studying the baking ingredients. "Baking is one thing I've never mastered."

She rolled up her sleeves. "Watch and learn, grasshopper."

"What?" He tilted his head.

"Never mind. Very old TV show."

"I'm off to take a shower."

Good. She had some thinking to do. As she measured ingredients and whipped them together, she thought about her father's case. Without a doubt, Buford had been in Misty Hollow on that fateful night. She still believed he had a hand in her father's death somehow. The problem would be proving it. Then, there was the list of people who worked for him. One of them would know something, even if they weren't aware of what they knew. That was the next problem. Having the time and weather to actually visit and question those people.

"Does it always snow this much in the winter?" She asked as Zeke, his hair wet from the shower, entered the kitchen.

"Not in a few years. You got lucky." He flashed a grin, poured himself another cup of coffee, and headed out of the room. "I'll be in my office if you need me."

Thank goodness he didn't think she needed entertaining. She might be staying temporarily in his home, but she didn't need him to hover.

Footsteps pounded on the front porch as she pulled the German chocolate cake from the oven. It would need to cool before it could be frosted. She set it on top of the stove and turned to stare into the grim face of Buford.

"What kind of game are you playing?" His lip curled in a snarl.

"I don't know what you mean?" She wet a rag and wiped down the counter.

"You here for my nephew's money?"

A laugh escaped her. She hadn't expected that comment at all. "Of course not. My place is too cold. I'm only staying until the weather clears. The weather has been bitterly cold. Rest assured, Mr. Matchett, I am not a gold digger." Rest assured, Mister. I'm digging for something far greater. Justice.

~

That's what Buford thought? That Shea was after his money? She wouldn't be the first woman to try and snare him, but his uncle's belief that she was made Zeke laugh. He took his empty mug to the kitchen.

"Shea isn't like that." He tossed her a wink. "She's a successful career woman who doesn't need a man or his money."

"Then she's lying." Buford crossed his arms and

glared. "All women are out to get what they can. Believe me, she's no different. That woman has an agenda. You just don't know it yet."

His uncle had no idea how close to the truth he was getting. "What do you need today? You already went over the books the other day."

He sent Shea another glare. "I thought maybe we could incorporate another vineyard's grapes with ours and come up with a new wine. Something blended with Muscadines."

"The idea has merit. Who owns the other vineyard?"

"I'm leaving that up to you." He returned his attention to Shea. "Why isn't that cake frosted yet?"

"It's too hot."

"Then cut me a piece without frosting."

Her face darkened. "I will not. You'll wait like everyone else."

His hands curled into fists.

Her eyes narrowed. "You may be bigger than I am, sir, but I'm a black belt in karate. Care to have a go?"

"A forceful woman isn't very desirable."

Shea smirked and marched from the kitchen. "The cake will be ready to frost in a while. Learn some patience."

"Come into the office," Zeke said. "We'll talk more about your idea."

Buford stared at the cake for a moment then marched over and smashed it flat. "I gave you the idea. You go with it if you want. I've other things to do."

Not for the first time, Zeke wanted to throttle his uncle. "That was wrong. You should stay away for a while."

"You can't keep me away."

"I can. You seem to forget this is my house, not to mention I have a deputy staying here. I could have you arrested for trespassing."

Buford stepped so close Zeke could smell the liquor on his breath. "Stop testing me, boy. Family or not, I'll put you down."

"That sounds like a threat."

"It's a promise." Buford stormed from the house, slamming the door behind him.

"I'd like nothing more than to arrest him." Shea headed back to the kitchen and stared at her ruined cake. She heaved a heavy sigh and scraped it into the garbage. "I really wanted him to be the one responsible for my father's death."

"We'll get him on something else. I'm really sorry about the cake."

"It was just a cake." She glanced toward the window. "Snow stopped. Think we could take a drive? I'd like to meet David Real."

"The headhunter? Why?"

"He used to work for Buford. The man might have some insight on whether your uncle is capable of hiring someone to kill my father."

"David lives in town, so it shouldn't be too hard to pay him a visit. He's most likely in his office. I've only met him once at a fundraiser to add a wing to the library. He wasn't very friendly. I'll grab my coat." Talking to Real would be a lot safer than crossing Buford. "I'll drive."

A few minutes later, he drove his old truck down Main Street until he reached the small white clapboard house converted into a business. He parked in one of the three parking spots and hurried to open Shea's door for her.

"Do you know what to say once we're inside?"

"The truth. That I'm asking what type of man Buford was to work for." She grinned up at him, stealing his breath. "I'll say that you and I are getting engaged, and I want to know what kind of family I'm marrying into. You can thank your uncle for the idea."

"That'll have Buford seeing red for sure." Zeke liked the idea. It would also keep other women from bothering him. He wasn't ready to settle down. Not yet, anyway.

"Come on in." David Real, a tall, thin man with a receding hairline, greeted them. "I gave the receptionist the day off. What can I do for you?" His gaze stayed on Shea a little longer than necessary.

Zeke put a protective hand on her lower back as Real led them to his office. "Shea has some questions she'd like to ask you."

The man's back stiffened. "Sure. It's a slow day." His smile remained in place as he sat at his desk. "Ask away."

Shea gave him another smile that made Zeke wish she wasn't playacting. "We're getting married and his uncle, Buford Matchett, well…" she managed to look sad, "seems a bit harsh, to put it mildly. I know you used to work for him ten years ago and was wondering whether you could share your thoughts about his character."

"The former mayor? That sounds like an odd request from someone getting ready to marry into the family." He steepled his fingers under his chin.

"Is it?" Shea widened her eyes in an innocent gaze. "I've been burned before, and it will devastate me if it happens again."

Zeke thought she laid it on a little thick, but Real seemed to be buying into her plea.

The man unfolded his hands and leaned his elbows on the desktop. "Buford Matchett is not a man to be messed with. He's mean with a fondness for whiskey. Not that there's anything wrong with a drink now and then, but the man is a drunk. Oh, he managed to hide it well from most, but I saw through him. If I were you, Miss Sydney, I'd run as fast and far from him as I could."

Shea's features hardened. "I didn't tell you my last name."

"Everyone knows who you are." He grinned, the smile not quite reaching his eyes. "You're the new deputy. There aren't many secrets in this town. You'll learn that soon enough."

Zeke stood and pulled Shea to her feet. "Thank you for your time, sir. I'll make sure my uncle doesn't cause too many problems for my fiancée."

"Good luck with that, Matchett." The man's laugh followed them outside.

Something close to dread trickled down Zeke's spine. Why did he feel as if they'd just made everything worse?

Chapter Nine

That didn't go as planned. Shea sat across a table in the diner from Zeke who stared at his large soda.

"I'm sorry for dragging you into all this." Shea'd made a big mess of everything. She'd come to Misty Hollow believing Buford guilty of her father's death, questioned a man who would most likely go straight to Buford about the visit, and pretended to be engaged to Zeke. All for what? She didn't know anything more than when she'd arrived in town. Some deputy she'd turned out to be.

"It's fine, at least for the moment." His tone said the opposite. "I don't think Real believed the engagement story, and my uncle will know about this within the hour. I guarantee it."

She nodded and took a sip of her soda. "I should probably move back where I came from."

"Don't do that." He reached across the table and put his hand over hers. "You're going to help me prove that Buford is stealing from me."

She sighed. "Okay." She needed to let go of her quest for revenge and do her job. Be the good deputy she knew she was. Helping Zeke would help her let her go of her father's case. The thought stabbed her heart. She'd so wanted to find his killer. Had really thought she'd found the man. "Show me the books when we get back to your place."

Sirens wailed outside. The sheriff's car and another sped past the diner. Shea bolted to her feet. "I need to go."

"I'll have to drive you." Zeke tossed some money on the table and raced outside behind her.

Shea called the office for details.

"Active shooter," Doris said. "Supermarket. All hands on deck."

"On my way." Shea hung up and told Zeke where to take her.

The sheriff met them as soon as they pulled up to the barricades. "Sorry, Zeke, but Buford has been shot." He motioned to a man in the parking lot. "He isn't dead, but every time we try to go to him, the shooter inside the store takes a shot at us."

"Why?" Zeke paled.

"Some kind of argument. You'll have to stay here. Deputy, come with me."

Shea skirted around the barricade and followed the sheriff to where the other deputies congregated. "What does the shooter want?"

"No idea. No one answers the phone inside."

She glanced at the others' uniforms. "Graham and I are in plainclothes. Maybe we can sneak in through a side door as customers and take out the shooter."

Deputy Young held up her phone. "It's the shooter. She wants Zeke Matchett."

She? Zeke? Shea turned to where he stood, a worried expression on his face. "Why?"

"Didn't say. Only that if Zeke isn't inside within

five minutes, she'll shoot someone."

"He cannot go in alone. I'll sneak around back while the shooter's attention is on Zeke." She waited for the sheriff to agree then went to get Zeke.

He looked stunned. "Do we know who it is?"

"No. Don't worry. I'll be inside with you. Deputy Young, go to the sheriff. Once Zeke enters the building, you might be able to reach Buford." She nodded to Graham, and they sprinted to the side of the building.

Shea spotted a door. Please be unlocked. She reached for the handle. The door swung open, and she stepped into a well air-conditioned stockroom. She pointed to a rolling garage-type door then a smaller one to the side of it.

Graham nodded and pulled his weapon.

Squaring her shoulders, Shea slowly opened the door. A frightened worker started to say something. Shea put a finger to her lips and shook her head. From the front of the store, a woman wailed and cursed. Otherwise, the store remained eerily silent.

"Why her and not me, Zeke?" The woman's question lured Shea to the front of the store. Zeke stood there, inches from a woman with black hair.

A gasp from one of the workers broke the silence.

The dark-haired shooter quickly stepped behind Zeke, using him as a shield and pulling him away from the door and windows. She aimed her Glock at his head. "Put down the guns, Deputies. We don't want anyone else to get hurt."

A muscle ticked in Zeke's jaw. "Let all these people go, Amber, and you and I can talk."

Mascara left black stripes down her cheeks. "Nothing matters anymore."

Shea set her service revolver on a shelf and put her hands up, her eyes studying the room. Men, women, and children were huddled together in the middle aisle, every face clouded with fear. Out the window, officers paced the edge of the lot. Officer Johnson aimed a rifle toward the store, waiting for a clear shot.

"Everything matters, Amber."

She turned her gun on Shea. "Why her?"

Shea's mouth dropped open. "You think we're getting married? We're not. That was only a ruse to extract information out of someone."

"You lie!" Her eyes flashed. "Every woman wants Zeke. Why wouldn't they? Look at him."

Zeke's face reddened.

"He's handsome, kind, and rich. Why wouldn't you want him? Don't lie to me."

The woman was nuttier than a fruit bat. "I'm not lying. I haven't known Zeke long enough to want to be his wife."

"You're staying in his house." Her eyes narrowed. "Oh, Buford told me all about it before I shot him. I didn't plan on shooting him, but he made me mad. Said I wasn't good enough for Zeke and neither were you." She smirked. "I don't care what he thinks about you." Her finger squeezed the trigger.

Shea dove behind a display of soda cases. Cans exploded, covering her hair and clothes with sticky liquid. Another shot, a grunt, and Graham fell. Shea's eyes met Zeke's before Amber started pulling him toward the back of the store.

She couldn't let them escape. If Zeke left with Amber, he'd be killed.

~

"Where are we going?" He yanked free of her grasp. What he wanted to do was punch her.

"Some place where we can be alone until you come to your senses."

He'd come to his senses months ago, thankfully. She'd been his sommelier and girlfriend for over a year before his eyes opened to the fact that Amber Solely was an obsessive-compulsive person. When she'd started dictating his every move and what he could or couldn't do, he'd broken things off and fired her. Obviously, she still hadn't gotten over things.

"Don't try to run, or I'll shoot you then go back inside and finish off your girlfriend." She poked the gun barrel into his back. "Hurry, before somebody sees us."

He picked up the pace, ducked down an alley, and slid into Amber's waiting car. A mere second before she squealed tires away from the supermarket, he caught sight of Shea giving chase. Zeke watched through the side mirror as she stopped in the middle of the road. Thank you, God, she's still alive. He prayed his uncle and Graham would survive as well.

"This could have all been avoided." Amber whipped the wheel to the left and veered down a back street. "If only you could've seen what was right in front of you."

He had. Zeke exhaled sharply out his nose and stared out the passenger side window. The temptation to grab for the gun overwhelmed him. He held back because of the speed at which she drove. Dying in a car accident wasn't something he wanted.

She headed up the mountain, taking corners too fast. A few times the car came dangerously close to the edge of the road and sheer drop-offs.

"Why aren't you talking to me? We have issues to

resolve." She cut him a quick glance.

"I prefer your attention be on your driving." He clutched the handle above the door.

"Great. Now you're sulking."

It seemed like forever before she pulled up in front of a ramshackle hunting cabin—something the mountain had plenty of. "This place will work great as a place for us to talk." She motioned the gun for him to get out of the car.

Zeke contemplated running, but that would only earn him a bullet in the back. Amber might profess to love him, but she'd kill him rather than let him get away again. He shoved the door open and climbed out, shoving his hands into the pockets of his coat.

"I'm sure we can start a fire and warm up."

"You've been here before?"

"It belongs to the father of someone I went to high school with. No one uses it anymore. It's perfect." She linked her arm with his. "I'd forgotten how good this felt. Touching you."

It took all his strength not to shudder as she pressed close. Instead, he increased his pace, making her have to almost run to keep up with him.

Inside, firewood lay in a pile next to the rock fireplace. "Do you have a lighter?" He held out his hand.

She pulled one from her pocket then sat cross-legged on the dirty wooden floor, keeping the gun trained on him. If not for the weapon, it would seem a little like the times they spent together at the beginning of their relationship. Zeke doing something, Amber watching and chattering.

"Why would your fiancée deny getting married to you?"

"She isn't my fiancée. We barely know each other." He broke kindling into smaller pieces and put them teepee style in the fireplace.

"But, she's staying at your house."

"Because she's renting the little place at the end of the vineyard, and it's freezing. She's only staying until the weather warms a bit." He lit the fire, blew gently on the burning coal, then sat back.

"You're always so nice, Zeke." She rested her head on his shoulder. making him want to cringe again. "Except to me. Breaking up with me shattered my heart. That wasn't nice at all."

"I'm sorry to have hurt you, but we aren't meant for each other."

Her dark unblinking eyes stared at him, making him squirm. Finally, she said, "If I can't have you, no one will. I'm sure you know that."

He gave a slow nod. Eventually, she'd let down her guard a bit, and he'd go for the gun. If he lived that long. Either way, he had to try.

"Yes, I do. Let's just sit and let me think, okay? You can't really expect me to say yes immediately after you shot my uncle and the deputy, not to mention holding an entire grocery store hostage."

"Fine. It isn't as if anyone will find us here anyway. I'm sure you'll make the right choice. Then, we'll leave the state, the country even, and start over somewhere else. Just the two of us."

Not likely. He turned to face her, searching the lovely face for the woman he'd once thought he loved. Zeke saw nothing but insanity in her eyes now. Keeping his gaze locked on hers, he reached for the gun, shoving her away from him.

She screamed and cursed, raking his face with her fingernails.

He scuttled back, the gun clenched in his hand.

"Are you going to shoot me now? Well then, do it." She pulled the neckline of her shirt and coat down. "Right here in my broken heart."

"I don't want to shoot you." He shook his head. "I'm sorry, Amber. It will never work between us." Especially after today. "You need help. Let me take you to that help."

"To jail, you mean. Never." She lunged to her feet and raced out the door.

He gave chase, but she was in her car and speeding away before he caught up to her. Great. A crazy woman on the run, snow falling like crazy, and he had a very long walk until he would be somewhere with cell-phone reception.

He tucked the gun into the back of his waistband, pulled up the collar of his coat, and started down the mountain.

Chapter Ten

The cold stabbed his face. Zeke wrapped his arms tighter around his middle in a vain attempt to warm himself. He'd lost feeling in his feet a mile back and wondered how his eyes didn't freeze.

He hoped for a vehicle—anyone other than Amber—to stop and offer him a ride. No one was out on this frigid day. Not this high on the mountain anyway.

Tires crunched on the icy road. Zeke glanced back then dove into the bushes. Armed or not, he didn't want to be caught by Amber again. He wouldn't even be able to pull the trigger if things came down to it. Not on a woman he'd once loved.

He stayed hidden until she passed then ventured slowly back onto the road. Staying within the protection of the trees would be safer, but trudging through thick snow would slow him down. Zeke had one goal. Stay alive and get off the mountain. Maybe he'd be lucky enough to find a cabin with people living there.

Several times he had to hide as Amber circled back in search of him. She'd drive by at a crawl, her gaze searching the woods on each side of the road. With the trees devoid of leaves, finding a place to hunker down wasn't easy.

He shivered harder as a pine tree released its burden of snow down the neck of his coat. His teeth clattered. Zeke needed to find cell-phone service quick or it would be his corpse someone would discover come springtime.

He forced himself on. His heart leaped into his throat when he spotted the glimmer of a light through the trees across the road. A house or a mirage? Not bothering to search for the road leading to the place, he plunged through the trees, snow, and fallen branches until he stepped into a clearing.

"Hello, house." No one in their right mind would walk up on a mountain cabin without calling out first.

A man stepped onto the front porch that spanned the width of the house. A big dog sat next to him. "That you, Matchett?"

Thank God. "Yeah, Spencer, it's me. Mind if I come in and warm up? I'll tell you all about it. Do you have phone service?"

"Sure do. Come on. Sierra, put on a pot of coffee, would you?" He helped a shivering Zeke into the house and out of his coat. "Sit over there by the fire and take off those shoes."

Zeke's fingers barely managed the laces. Soon, shards of pain shot through his feet as they thawed. Spencer's wife thrust a cup of hot coffee into his hands before draping a quilt over his shoulder.

"Who do you want me to call?" She asked.

"Deputy Sydney at the sheriff's office."

She nodded and went to place the call.

"Want to tell me how you ended up on foot in the snow?" Spencer sat across from him. "Last time I found someone in the snow, I married her." He grinned.

He started with the supermarket shooting then

moved on to his abduction and escape. "I didn't think I'd make it out alive there for a while." He shifted and removed the gun from his waistband, setting it on a side table. "I managed to disarm her then thought I'd freeze to death. Sure am glad I found your place."

"You're lucky. My closest neighbor is five miles away."

"The deputy is coming," Sierra said, joining her husband on the sofa. "She sounded relieved to hear you were alive."

He smiled. "Did she mention my uncle?"

She shook her head. "I'm sure she'll tell you when she gets here. Shouldn't take her long. No more than half an hour."

Half an hour? He would never have made it down the mountain on foot in that time frame.

Warmed enough, he removed the quilt. "Thank you." He slipped his feet into his now dry shoes he'd placed on the hearth. "I couldn't appreciate your help more. Can I return the favor by delivering a few bottles of wine?"

"No need to repay us. It's our pleasure. Are you hungry? Sierra can whip you up a sandwich."

His stomach growled in response. "That would be great." True, the Thornes did what any respectable person would do, but they'd literally saved his life. He'd pay them for their kindness one way or another.

~

He'd heard about the shooting inside the supermarket. Glee had filled him when he'd been told one of the deputies had been shot. Regret poured through him when he discovered it hadn't been Deputy Sydney. All his troubles had almost been wiped away because of a crazy woman.

The whole town was in a frenzy because of Zeke's abduction. Good riddance was what he thought. Zeke had grown too big for his britches in his opinion.

He squirmed and pressed the button on the television remote to catch the news. A person couldn't know too much about what went on in their hometown.

Since the abductor had proven she wouldn't hesitate to pull the trigger, maybe he could hire her to rid Misty Hollow of Deputy Sydney. Heck, maybe she'd kill the deputy for free. He laughed and turned up the volume then popped a pain pill. His side was killing him.

Maybe he needed to call in the doctor. Yeah, it might not be a bad idea. He reached for the phone and called for help.

~

Shea drove as fast as she dared on the icy roads up the mountain. Zeke was alive and well! So much for professionalism. She'd been frantic with worry since seeing Amber drive off with him at the supermarket.

She rammed her truck into park and darted up the steps of the Thorne residence. A big dog barked and growled. "Oh, hush." Shea rapped on the door, praying she didn't lose a chunk of her backside.

A pretty woman with honey-colored hair opened the door. "You must be the deputy. Come on in. I'm Sierra. My husband is Spencer."

"I'm Shea. Thank you." She searched the room for Zeke, finding him standing next to the fireplace. "You're okay?"

"I'm good." He smiled.

"Would you like some coffee, Deputy?"

What she really wanted was to get Zeke safely

home. "That would be nice." It wouldn't hurt for Zeke to remain by the fire for a few more minutes. "How did you break free?"

He pointed to a gun. "I wrestled her for it."

"Where is she now?" Shea accepted the cup Sierra offered her.

"No idea. We played cat and mouse for a while until I found this place. Hopefully, she's long gone by now." He sat in a chair as Sierra handed him a sandwich.

Shea declined when offered one. "She needs to be behind bars. Thankfully, your uncle was only grazed along his ribcage. Deputy O'Connor required surgery but will pull through."

"That's good news. Sorry she escaped, but I couldn't shoot her."

No, a man as nice as Zeke would not be able to shoot another person. She finished her coffee, retrieved the gun Zeke had set on the table, and walked with him back to her truck. "Your truck is still parked where you left it. I had someone take me to get mine. We can pick it up first then head to the office to fill out the report."

"Sounds good." He smiled and slid in. "Thanks for coming."

She wanted to tell him how frightened she'd been, how much she considered him a friend, how she wondered what it would be like to be considered more than a friend to him. Instead, she smiled and started the truck. "Not a problem. The thought of spending another chilly night in bitter isolation in my rental had me speeding here."

"Very funny." He laughed.

"Are you sure you're okay? We could run by the hospital and have a doctor check you over."

"I will be going to see Buford, but I'm sure I'm fine."

Shea studied his face. He did seem as good as new. She couldn't force him to seek medical attention. Nodding, she turned around and drove back to the main road. A car sped past as she pulled from the Thornes' driveway, then slammed on its brakes, and spun to face them.

Shea met the crazed stare of Amber. This would not be good.

The other car's engine revved.

Shea backed her truck into the drive then turned to speed in the other direction. "Hold on. This will be a hairy ride." No one in their right mind would take part in a high-speed chase on icy mountain roads, yet here they were. "Get Amber's gun and aim for her tires."

"I can't do that." He frowned. "What if she crashes?"

"Better her than us." She shot him a sharp glance. "I'd do it, but I'm trying to keep us alive."

Amber's car loomed in the rearview mirror right before she rammed into the rear of the truck. Shea tightened her grip on the steering wheel as the truck fishtailed. "Do it!"

He growled and rolled down the window. With the gun in one hand, he hung out and fired.

A bullet pinged the truck. The woman had another gun. Things had gone from bad to worse. "Get back in here before she shoots you."

"No need to tell me twice." He put the gun in the glove compartment and reattached his seatbelt as Shea veered around a corner, and the truck slid toward a steep embankment.

One tire hung over before the other three gained traction, and they were able to stay on the road. Perspiration ran down her back despite the winter cold. "Call the sheriff. See if he can send us some help. Maybe meet us on the other side of this mountain."

Zeke nodded and pulled his cell phone from his pocket. "No service."

There were definite downsides to country living. "Keep checking. Place the call as soon as you can."

Her knuckles ached from her grip on the steering wheel. Amber came in for another hit. This one sent the truck toward the mountain and the car behind them skidding toward a cliff. Shea tore her eyes away from the scene behind them and focused on the road in front of them. They'd know soon enough whether Amber still followed.

She careened around the corner seconds after they did. The woman seemed as good of a driver as Shea, and Shea had training. Finally, the road dipped downward. They'd be out of this hellish adventure soon.

To think she'd been worried about Buford coming after her. Instead, it was a jealous ex-girlfriend of Zeke's. "Hopefully, we live through this, so we can find out how your uncle is stealing from you."

"I know how. He's using a fake name similar to one of the companies we deal with." Zeke glanced over his shoulder. "She's coming up on us again. What I need to prove is how much money, where the money is, and why he's stealing from a company he partially owns. The deeper we dig, the angrier he'll get."

"Let him." He might not be the one who murdered her father, but she would help Zeke find the truth.

Two squad cars waited at the foot of the mountain.

The tension left Shea's body in a whoosh.

"Amber turned around." Zeke looked in the side mirror. "They won't catch her."

"I have a feeling this isn't the last we've seen of her."

Chapter Eleven

After taking Zeke's statement at the department, Shea drove them to the hospital so he could check on Buford. Fraught with danger, the day's events weighed her down with exhaustion. Shea rolled her head on her shoulders. Sleep was still a few hours away. She wasn't the only tired one in the truck. Zeke looked ready to fall over.

"You sure you want to do this?"

He nodded. "I need to see that he's okay. My uncle might not be the nicest guy on earth, but he's all the family I have right now, and it was my former girlfriend who shot him."

"Okay." She found a parking spot not too far from the hospital building and shoved her door open. At least it had stopped snowing.

Inside, she flashed her badge, then a nurse led them down a long hall. They stepped aside as a gurney carrying David Real pushed past. He gave them a feeble wave and groaned.

The nurse stopped in front of room 105. "He's resting and stable. Should be coherent by now."

"Thank you." Zeke entered first, Shea close behind. "How are you, Buford?"

His eyes opened. "Feel like I've been shot. You don't have much luck with the ladies, do you?" He glared at Shea. "Is it true the two of you are getting hitched?"

"No, sir, it was merely a ploy to force information out of someone." Thankfully, the room held two chairs and she lowered into one, leaving the other for Zeke.

"I was told the bullet only grazed you." Zeke sat.

"I still got shot. Laid in the snow like an abandoned dog. You look like hell. What happened to you?" His eyes widened as Zeke told him of his abduction. "Well, it looks like you had a worse day than I did. Thanks for bringing him, Deputy, and I'm glad you aren't getting married."

Zeke shook his head. "I hope to marry someday, Uncle. You'll have to wrap your mind around that." He stood. "We'll talk when you are released." He patted the man's other shoulder and left the room.

"Hold on, Deputy. Who were you pulling info from?"

"David Real." She bit back a smile at the shocked look on Buford's face.

"Why?" The words came out like a growl.

"I thought you were responsible for my father's death. And I'm not completely convinced you're totally innocent, but at least I know you didn't pull the trigger. Have a good evening." She left him with shock on his face.

"Do you think it wise to tell him you're suspicious?" Zeke tilted his head.

"Keeps him on his toes." She laughed and headed back toward the front of the hospital. "Let's get out of here. I'm tired, I'm hungry, and I want that big guest bed of yours. Want to pick up Chinese takeout?"

He put a hand to his chest. "Gasp. You aren't going to eat a salad?"

"Hush." Grinning, she opened the door to her truck. "I really am glad Amber didn't kill you."

"That makes two of us." He returned her smile and climbed in.

Shea pulled into the drive-thru of the town's only Chinese food place, gave their order, and pulled into an empty parking spot to wait for someone to bring out their order. "I've been thinking about your uncle embezzling. You should just confront him. Show him what you've found and see what he says."

"Maybe. I sure dread the confrontation though."

"You disarmed a crazy person with a gun. I'm sure you can handle your uncle." She rolled down her window as their food arrived. "What's the worse he can do? Yell at you? If he hits you, then you can charge him with assault."

"Okay, Deputy." His stomach growled loud enough for her to hear. "I wasn't aware how hungry I was until smelling this."

"Then, let's take you home, sir." She backed from the spot and headed to his place as fast as the icy roads allowed.

Before eating, she headed to her room and changed into the baggy clothes she slept in. By the time she returned to the dining room, Zeke had also changed and had set the food out on the table.

"Feel like watching a movie after we eat?" He handed her a plate. "I have a theater room."

Of course, he did. "Not really. I want to eat and go to bed." She put a healthy serving of kung pao chicken on her plate. "Thought you'd feel the same."

"I can't sleep right after I eat. I'll need some time to wind down. Maybe I'll spend the time figuring out what to say to my uncle when he arrives in a day or two."

"Good idea." She didn't envy him the task, but that was something Zeke needed to do. Best to get it over and done with. "Maybe you can buy out his share. That way he has no say or right to the books or any other part of the vineyard."

"I've given it some thought."

"It's really none of my business, but you did ask for my help." She forked a mouthful of her supper into her mouth. A slight burn hit the back of her throat. Just the way she liked it.

"I did ask, and I value your opinion. Friends listen to friends."

"Is that what we are?"

"Isn't it? I wouldn't let just anyone sleep under my roof."

"Sure, you would. Nice guy, remember?" She could only hope his niceness wouldn't be a danger.

~

Buford breezed through Zeke's office door two days later. He eyed the ledger on the desktop. "You doing my job?"

"I'm taking away your job." Zeke forced his expression to remain firm. "How can you steal from me? From the company your father founded?"

"It's not stealing if it's yours." His face darkened.

"Then why make up a false name so close to the real company name that I didn't catch it until I took a good hard look?" Zeke jabbed the ledger with his finger. "I'm going to buy you out, Buford. I don't want your hands in any part of this vineyard."

"You aren't buying me out of anything!" He planted his palms firmly on the desk and leaned close. Whiskey fumes wafted over Zeke's face. "You will continue to give me my share. Other than that, I won't darken your doorstep again. Got it?"

"That works for me." Zeke's jaw clenched. "I knew you were capable of a lot of things but not this. And don't you dare go take it out on Sybil."

"I'll do what I please with my wife. Keep your nose out of my business. I still have friends in high places, and I can ruin you, boy." He whipped around and marched from the office.

Zeke heaved a heavy sigh. His hands trembled. Shea would be proud of him. He'd stood his ground, even though he'd hated every second of the confrontation. The sound of glass shattering drew him to the window.

Buford brought up a hand holding a tire iron and brought it down across the windshield of Zeke's truck. Once that had shattered, he moved to the next window, then the next. When he finished with the windows, he slashed the tires. Then, as the finale, he shot up his middle finger toward the house before climbing into his truck.

Shaking his head, Zeke called the mechanic who promised to bring a tow truck. Once he got his truck back, Zeke would be keeping it in the garage next to the Mercedes.

Jo, the owner of the garage, arrived twenty minutes later with the tow truck. Zeke grabbed his coat from the back of a chair and stepped outside to meet him.

"Who did this?" Jo stared at the carnage.

"Buford."

"You going to press charges?"

"Wouldn't do any good."

Jo tsked. "Probably right about that. We'll get her fixed up, but it'll be a couple of weeks. Need a loaner?"

"No. I have another car." He really liked the truck, though.

An hour after Jo towed the truck away, Shea stopped in front of the house. She climbed from her truck and stomped inside the house.

"What do you mean Buford vandalized your truck?" She put her hands on her hips. "Are you going to press charges?"

"No, I'm not. He'd been drinking and got upset when I told him I didn't want him on the property anymore. When he cools down, Buford will pay for the damages."

"You act as if you've had this experience before."

"I have. My worry is about his wife. She usually takes the brunt of his anger."

"I'll go by to check on her."

"You might as well come in and let me fix you something for lunch."

She shook her head. "I'll buy something in town. Please reconsider pressing charges. You've now let him get away with vandalism and theft. Sometimes, you can't be nice."

As much as he valued her opinion, this time she'd stepped over the line. "I'll do as I please with my family. See you later. You don't need to check on my aunt. I'll give her a call."

Hurt flickered in her eyes. Without a word, she exited the house.

Zeke was on a roll. He'd hurt two people in one day, and it was barely noon. How was that for being nice?

His shoulders sagged as he returned to his office to organize the books in the way he preferred. One more thing on an already full plate. During the busy season, having Buford do the ledger had helped immensely. Zeke still hadn't hired a sommelier and needed to before the weather turned nice. Hire a chef and staff to get his restaurant up and running, or something that offered food to those touring the winery. Hiring an accountant wouldn't hurt either. He loved running the vineyard, but the business side of it would be best left to someone else.

Back in his office, he dialed the number to Buford's house.

"Hello?" Sybil's timid voice drifted through the phone line.

"It's Zeke. Are you okay?"

"Why wouldn't I be?"

"I upset Buford and don't want him to take it out on you." He settled into his leather office chair.

"He isn't home. If he's mad, then he's tying one on at the bar. Don't you know better than to anger him?"

"If he starts hitting you, call me right away. I mean it. I can be there in twenty minutes if I push it."

"Then he'll start on you."

"I can take it, Sybil." He closed his eyes against the pain in her voice. "Why do you stay with him?"

"He's my husband. I love him. He loves me in his way. Goodbye, Zeke. Have a nice day." She hung up.

Thankfully, Zeke's parents had shown him what love really was. If love was what Sybil and his uncle had, he wanted no part of it.

He redid the past year's numbers then closed the ledger and locked it away. A glance at the clock let him know Shea would be home soon, and he wanted to cook her something for supper as an apology.

He was elbow deep in zucchini lasagna. The thought of it made him want to gag, but he knew she'd appreciate the effort he put in to make a healthier meal.

The front door opened.

"I'm in here," he called out.

She peeked into the kitchen. "In a better mood now?"

"I'm sorry." He held up his hands, one dripping with tomato sauce. "I had a rough morning and took it out on you."

"Like you said, it's your family. I won't do anything you don't want me to."

He washed his hands before answering. "Every decision I make regarding Buford has to be made with his wife in mind."

"I understand."

The phone rang. By the third ring, Zeke's hands were dried. "Hello?"

"I need you." Sybil's plea sounded barely above a whisper. "He's worse than ever."

Chapter Twelve

It had taken a bit of trouble, but he'd finally found out how to contact the psycho woman. The phone rang and rang. Just as he was ready to slam his phone down, she answered.

"Who is this?"

"I'd rather not divulge that information. I have a job for you that will pay quite well."

"Keep talking."

Her belligerent tone rankled. Women should not try to control any situation over a man. "There's a certain female deputy I need disposed of. You've proven you have no qualms about pulling the trigger on anyone."

Silence screamed for several seconds. "How will I get to her?"

"That's up to you to find out, but you could start by bugging every phone that has to do with Zeke Matchett."

She laughed. "That's already been done. You obviously know I'm not an idiot or you wouldn't have contacted me. While he was at the hospital, I had plenty of time. I'll call you at this number when the job is done." She hung up on him.

He glared at the phone before setting it on his desk. Maybe he should've taken care of things himself rather than deal with such a woman, but removing himself as far as possible when the deputy was killed seemed the wisest choice.

He couldn't allow his rage to interfere with the final plan. His pent-up anger would find the usual punching bag.

"I have to go." Zeke grabbed his coat and headed for the door.

"Go where?" Shea automatically reached for her coat.

"You don't need to go, but my aunt is calling for help."

"Then I absolutely have to go." She slipped her arms through the holes. "You could be going into a domestic dispute." Adrenaline burned through her veins. This was so much like what she'd read about in the files regarding her father's death. She followed Zeke into the garage. "We should take my truck. You put chains on the wheels."

"Right." He opened the garage door. Frigid air slapped her in the face. "As long as we hurry."

They rushed to her vehicle. Shea made a quick call to the department stating where they were going and that she would call for backup if the situation warranted.

"I'm headed home," Sheriff Westbrook said. "I'll check on my wife then head to the Matchetts' place. If you don't need me, give me a call, and I'll turn around and return home. Do not be a hero."

"Yes, sir." With his wife close to giving birth, he checked on her several times a day.

She glanced at Zeke over the hood of the truck as he slid into the truck. Worry creased his face. The fact he didn't open the door for her as he usually did, confirmed he was more frightened than he let on.

Driving as fast as she deemed safe, they arrived at Buford's house in less than thirty minutes. Too long of a response time. How did people on the mountain stay safe in the winter?

"Hold on." She stopped Zeke from rushing from the car. "I need to assess the situation."

"There's nothing to assess." He glowered. "My uncle is in there threatening my aunt as we speak." Zeke shoved open his door.

"He can't do a whole lot with a bullet graze in his side. It required stitches." Shaking her head, she followed Zeke to the front porch and knocked, shoving her coat aside to make her weapon accessible.

After several knocks, Buford yanked open the door hard enough to put a hole in the wall behind it. "What do you want?"

"We got a call from this residence asking for—"

"Let me talk to Sybil." Zeke stepped in front of her.

"She call you?" His brow furrowed. "The old lady's nothing but a whiner. I haven't laid a hand on her."

"May we speak to your wife, sir?" Shea made her tone as firm as possible.

A woman with a tear-streaked face peered around Buford. "I'm fine. Thank you for coming. I, uh, thought we had an intruder and Buford was sleeping and well…"

"Ma'am, may we speak with you in private?" Shea knew all too well from her years on the force that most abused women wouldn't press charges. Especially after their husband calmed down.

"It's late." She gave a trembling smile. "We're getting ready for bed. There's really nothing to concern yourself with."

"Mr. Matchett." Shea squared her shoulders. "If I find out you're beating your wife, I won't hesitate to put your sorry body in prison. Good evening, Mr. and Mrs. Matchett."

"Don't threaten me, little girl. You'd be on the losing end."

"Threatening a law enforcement officer is not a game you should play." Shea gave a thin smile. If she needed something to charge him with, it wouldn't be hard. She turned to leave then stopped and looked back. "Oh, and it's not a threat, sir. It's a promise." With a nod, she continued toward her truck.

The first shot spun her like a top, the second dropped her to her knees.

Zeke yelled and threw himself across her.

Buford, eyes wide, shoved his wife inside and slammed the door.

If Shea needed further proof that Buford did not kill her father, she had it now. The shots hadn't come from Buford's direction. The man's fear had been palpable, and he'd shielded his wife.

"Off." She groaned and rolled Zeke off of her before reaching for her gun. "Call the sheriff. Get us some backup."

Fire burned through her left shoulder and left thigh. Still, she needed to see where the shots had come from and return fire if necessary. She blinked away the spots in front of her eyes.

Zeke placed the call, took off his coat and his shirt, and put his coat back on. "You're bleeding." He ripped his shirt into two bandages. "Let me at least try and stop the bleeding until help arrives."

"In the house!" Buford waved to them from the side

of his porch. "Hurry up."

Shock whipped through Shea. The man wanted to help them?

Zeke scooped Shea into his arms and ran in a zigzag pattern across the snow-covered lawn. A bullet kicked up the powder at his feet.

Despite the pain, Shea chuckled. "Where'd you learn that move? The movies?"

"Yep." His chest rumbled. He didn't release her until they were inside. "Thank you, Uncle."

"Couldn't let some freak kill my only nephew. Put her on the table. Sybil, see what you can do." He grabbed a rifle from over the mantel. "I'll watch over the place."

"The last thing we need is a shootout." Zeke lay Shea on the dining room table the second Sybil had it cleared. "Call an ambulance, please."

She nodded, her eyes wide in a pale face, and grabbed the phone receiver off the kitchen wall. "Shots fired at the Matchett place on the mountain. A deputy down. Shooter is still active. Sheriff is on the way. Need an ambulance." Sybil set the phone down without hanging up. "I used to be a dispatcher." She shrugged and grabbed a handful of dishtowels from a drawer. "Take her coat off, Zeke."

Shea hissed as he gently maneuvered her out of her coat. "Don't cut it off. It's the only one warm enough for this place." She bit her tongue as he pulled her arm free.

"Now, leave the room so I can remove her pants. It's started snowing again. We don't know how long it will take an ambulance to get here, and I need to clean the wounds." Sybil took a pair of kitchen shears from a drawer.

Shea had never missed the city more than at that

moment.

~

"I don't want to leave." Zeke's gaze focused on Shea.

She waved a dismissive hand. "I don't want you seeing me without my pants. Give a girl some privacy."

Leaving her was the hardest thing he'd ever had to do. He joined Buford at the window and took the other gun from over the mantel in his hands. Zeke stared at it in disgust.

"Stop being a sissy and help me find this moron." Buford shook his head and made a noise in his throat as he peered through a slit in the curtains. "It's hard to see with the heavy snowfall."

"It's going to take the ambulance a while." Which was why Zeke preferred living in the valley. His heart lurched at the thought of how much blood soaked his coat. "Do you have anything else I can wear?"

"Coat closet. Give that to Sybil to clean. If she doesn't stay busy, she'll be scared."

It was surprising Buford showed compassion for his wife. How could he resort to violence and harm her? It didn't make sense.

Zeke found a coat in the closet and laid it across a chair to wear when they left. He set the stained one on top of the washing machine past the kitchen. The sound of a bullet whizzing through the dining room window brought a scream from Sybil.

Zeke raced to the dining room. "Anyone hit?"

"No." Shea pointed. "Hit the wall. I'd like off the table please. Keep your eyes off me since I don't have on any pants."

Zeke helped her to the floor. One long, shapely leg

was wrapped in a towel with pink flamingos. It took some willpower for him to lift his eyes back up to her face. "Sorry. Stay down." He moved to the window, plastering his back against the wall and peering through the window.

Pain etched across her face as, weapon in hand, Shea crawled to the other side of the window. "Surely, you didn't think I'd lie there helpless."

He should've known better. With the bleeding relatively stopped, she'd want to be in the center of the action.

"You look good with a gun in your hand." She grinned. "Manly."

"A person doesn't need a gun in order to be a man." He started to take offense, but the twinkle in her eye told him she was joking. "I'm actually a good hunter. People are different. I don't want to shoot a person."

"I understand. It's a horrible experience."

"Look." He stiffened and jerked his chin toward the dark form of a person with a rifle darting past Shea's truck. "I think it's Amber."

"How would she know we were here?" She limped to the phone on the wall and removed the earpiece. "No bugs." She widened her eyes. "Which means, your phone might be tapped. I know you said she worked for you, stole from you, but is it possible you gave her a key to your house?"

"No. Only the winery." But, it wouldn't have been too difficult for her to have a copy made. Amber had been in his house many times, and he left his keys on the table in the foyer. "She got one somehow."

"Don't jump to conclusions. We'll have someone sweep your house when we leave here." She leaned heavily against the table.

A few minutes later, the roar of a snowmobile let them know Amber had left. Zeke shot his uncle a look. "You didn't hear her coming?"

"Things were loud in here." He rubbed both hands down his face. "I was yelling. You hurt me bad, boy. It's going to take a while to get over it."

"You were stealing." Zeke returned the gun to the mantel and frowned as his uncle poured a drink. Thank goodness, he'd been relatively sober when he and Shea arrived. If Buford had been drunk, he would most likely have assaulted the deputy. "Anyway, it's Amber, the woman from the supermarket who shot at us."

"You sure know how to pick 'em. Since you know who, why don't you know where?"

"The sheriff sent deputies by her last known address." Shea slowly lowered to the sofa, her left arm covered by a blue and white striped towel sling. A spot of blood had started to bleed through. "She wasn't there. No sign of where she went."

Flashing red and blue lights cut through the snow. The cavalry had arrived. Zeke opened the door for the sheriff and paramedics.

"Deputy Sydney." He rushed into the living room. His eyes widened at the sight of her bare legs then his features darkened. "How many times were you shot?"

"Two. Sorry about the undress, but it's only legs." She closed her eyes and winced as the paramedics lifted her onto a gurney. "We believe the shooter to be Amber Solely, and Zeke's home phone may be tapped."

"I'll send someone over to check the place." The sheriff put a hand on her right shoulder. "If you've survived this long, you'll be okay."

"Sure. Once the pain goes away." She held out a hand to Zeke. "Stay here until I'm released. She's still out there."

No way. Staying with Shea was worth the risk of a bullet.

Chapter Thirteen

The ride to the hospital seemed eternal. Shea's arm and leg burned and throbbed. Don't be a hero, the sheriff had said. She hadn't been, but keeping guard at the dining room window with Zeke hadn't helped her any.

She closed her eyes while the ambulance made its way down the mountain and didn't open them again until they stopped at the hospital in Langley. Misty Hollow had nothing more than a clinic to serve its citizens.

"What do people do when they have a heart attack," she mumbled as they wheeled her outside.

"Pardon?" The paramedic peered into her face. "You're having a heart attack?"

"No, just talking out loud." She gritted her teeth against the pain of being jostled.

"Law enforcement officer with multiple gunshot wounds," the paramedic told a waiting nurse. "Vitals are stable."

They wheeled her to a room and hoisted her from the gurney to a hospital bed. She groaned and tried not to pass out or throw up.

"Sorry, sweetie." The nurse patted her uninjured arm. "No more bouncing around." She stuck an oxygen monitor on Shea's finger. "Let's get you out of those clothes and into a gown so I can start an IV. It will help with the pain."

"Can you talk?" Sheriff Westbrook hovered by the curtain.

"As soon as I'm changed." Shea bit back a groan as her shirt was pulled over her head. Once she wore the thin hospital gown, she called for the sheriff to come in.

"We'll make it quick. I'm sure the doctor won't be long." He pulled a pad of paper from inside his coat. "Tell me what happened, start to finish."

Shea started with Zeke receiving the phone call from his aunt and ended with Amber leaving on a snowmobile. "Any luck finding bugs in Zeke's house?"

"Can't get anyone in until the morning." He patted her hand. "You'll be fine, Deputy. I'll post Deputy O'Connor outside your door."

"You really think Amber will return?"

"The woman has some kind of vendetta against you. She might try." He exited as the doctor entered.

After a thorough examination, Shea was prepped for surgery to remove the bullet in her upper arm. Great. She'd be out of work for a while.

When she woke up in an actual hospital room instead of a cubicle, Zeke dozed in a chair. She should've known he wouldn't stay behind regardless of the possible danger to himself.

"I told you to stay at Buford's."

He opened his eyes. "I don't always do what I'm told."

"This is getting serious." She pressed the button to raise the bed.

"Looks to me like Amber wants to kill you not me."

"Not true. It's you she kidnapped."

He shrugged. "Let's not banter. I'm staying close to you and that's it. The sheriff said you're to stay away from the department for at least five days."

"Okay."

"You aren't going to argue?"

"No. This will give me time to dig through my father's case files again. Now that I'm not fixated on Buford, there might be something I've missed that would lead me to the real killer." While Amber's MO today had been eerily similar to ten years ago, she doubted a teenager would have taken that fatal shot, and Amber would have been too young.

She gasped. How would Amber have known to recreate that day? Was it a coincidence? Too far-fetched. It had to be a coincidence, right?

"What's whirling in your head?" Zeke moved his chair closer to the bed. "You should be resting."

"I'm fine. The pain meds are great. Do you think Amber could've acted on the orders of someone else today? I mean, is she really that infatuated with you that she'd try to kill me?"

"I'm just that awesome." He gave a lopsided grin. "How can you be sure she doesn't want me dead too?"

"You'd have been shot on that mountain when she had you alone."

"Given time, she would have." He took her hand in his, his thumb rubbing against the back of hers. "I suppose she could be working for someone, but that would mean whoever is using her is scared of you."

"The person who killed my father."

"Possibly." He leaned over and kissed her forehead. "Go to sleep. I'll be right here when you wake up."

With the touch of his lips lingering on her skin, her

eyes drifted closed.

~

"You'll have to try again. Sneak into the hospital somehow. Figure it out."

"You aren't very appreciative," Amber said on the other end of the line. "I escaped minutes before the sheriff arrived. To gain access to the hospital would require some effort and planning."

He rolled his eyes. "Kill the girl, and you'll have Matchett all to yourself."

She laughed. "At this point, after his heroic act of trying to shield her body while she lay on the ground, he has to die too." She hung up on him for the second time.

Insolence. He wouldn't tolerate it in his regular employees, so why was he allowing this snippet of a woman to get away with doing so? Because she was the means to an end for him. Once the deputy was out of the picture, he didn't care what happened to Matchett, and he'd make sure Amber was arrested for the deeds.

He rubbed his hands together. He'd be in the clear. No one would be left to start digging up facts from ten years ago.

~

Amber entered the hospital, head down in scrubs she'd purchased from a Walmart. She carried a clipboard to hide the fact she wasn't wearing a badge then entered the doors that separated the ER from the rest of the hospital and moved as if she had somewhere to be quickly. Hospitals had emergencies all the time. No one would think twice about a nurse almost running down the halls.

The hard part would be finding the deputy's room, but she lucked out when the elevator door opened. She turned and pretended to study the clipboard when the sheriff exited the elevator. She was too close to her goal to get caught now.

She paused as the door to the elevators opened on the third floor. A deputy sat in a chair beside an open door and read a book. Bingo. By now, her picture had most likely been sent to every law enforcement office in the state. Waltzing into Deputy Sydney's room was impossible. She needed to lure the deputy and the other nurses away.

All Amber needed was two minutes. She put her hand in her pocket and grasped the syringes. One minute for the deputy and another for Zeke.

She strolled in and out of rooms looking for someone on life support. She found an old man who looked old enough to have been around when Jesus walked the earth. Amber pulled a separate syringe from her other pocket and ejected the liquid into the man's IV. It wouldn't be long now.

While she waited for the alarm to sound, she entered the nearest restroom. The alarm for code blue rang out a few minutes later. She rushed from the room, one hand in her pocket.

She skid to a halt when the deputy lifted his head, and his eyes collided with hers. Recognition flashed.

Plans foiled, Amber whipped around and raced for the stairs at the end of the hall, the deputy not far behind.

"Solely is in the hospital." He spoke into his radio. "I'm giving chase headed toward the stairs. Send backup. Halt!"

Amber kept going and pushed gurneys, food trays, and any other obstacles she came across into the hall. She shattered the glass containing an ax, barged through the doors leading to the stairs, and held them closed with the ax.

Her pounding feet echoed as she thundered downstairs. This time she got away with it, but the deputy would have someone with her the next time.

~

"Amber was here?" Zeke's blood chilled. "In the hospital?" He sagged in the chair.

"Yep. I chased her to the stairs, but she barricaded them. By the time backup arrived, she was long gone." O'Connor turned as the sheriff entered the room.

"What kind of security do you have at your place?"

"The best. I could hire another security guard, I guess."

Zeke couldn't keep Shea safe by himself. He would never have guessed Amber could be so formidable.

"Maybe some guard dogs, too." The sheriff glanced at the sleeping Shea. "There's more to this than a jealous ex, isn't there?"

How much should he say? He looked down at Shea. She'd probably be angry with him, but the sheriff needed to know.

"Her father was murdered ten years ago." He placed his hand over hers.

"I read about it."

"Shea thought my uncle murdered her father because of an altercation they'd had earlier that day. After going through the case files, she came here. We now know that there's no way Buford could have been the one. Shea's back to square one." He met the hard look of the sheriff. "She's toying with the idea that Amber might be working for the person responsible. Kill the deputy, stop the problem."

The sheriff frowned. "Did you ever suspect this woman of being capable of murder?"

"No." He shook his head. "She was clingy as far as the relationship went, but when she stole from the company, I fired her. Until the day at the supermarket, we hadn't spoken to each other. That started with a ruse that Shea and I were getting married." He shrugged. "A ploy to get information out of David Real who used to work for my uncle. Anyway, that's how Amber found out. Now, she doesn't believe us when we tell her the truth."

"This is the most convoluted thing I've heard in a while." The sheriff rubbed his hands down his face. "I'm beat. I'll think about all this after a few hours of sleep. At this point, we know that Miss Solely is capable of murder and won't stop until we stop her or she's fulfilled her mission."

"I didn't want him to know." Shea's eyes fluttered open. "He'll most likely fire me now."

"I'm sorry, but we're going to need help." Tomorrow, he'd call the animal shelter to see whether they had some dogs that would be good for security. "Keeping you safe is turning into a full-time job."

She smirked. "I can take care of myself."

"You're impossible."

"But you love me anyway," she murmured as her eyes drifted closed.

Did he love her? He doubted she'd remember her statement once the medication had worn off.

Zeke sat back in the chair and studied her pale face. Did he love this beautiful, tough, stubborn woman? He definitely had stronger feelings for her than any other woman he'd met.

Wouldn't that be his luck? He'd find the perfect woman only to have someone take her away?

Chapter Fourteen

Shea insisted on being released the next morning. Neither of her wounds were life-threatening. Now, she lay on Zeke's sofa halfway regretting her decision.

"You're in pain." Zeke stood over her.

"Of course, I am. I got shot." She smirked, trying to hide exactly how much pain she was in. What she wanted to do was take a pain pill and go to bed. What she did instead was sit, gun close at hand, while two men roamed the house in search of electronic bugs. Shea had no doubt in her mind Amber would come back to finish what she'd started. Especially if Shea's assumptions were correct, and the woman was doing someone else's bidding.

On the day of his abduction, Amber had been fixated on Zeke. Now, she seemed consumed with killing Shea. The person responsible for her father's death was running scared and wanted Shea out of the way and didn't mind using a mentally ill woman to do so.

"Phone lines were tapped." One of the men entered the room. "We didn't find any hidden cameras or bugs anywhere else. I'll let the sheriff know."

Zeke showed the men out before returning to Shea. "You can go to bed now."

"I'll rest here. So, Amber heard your aunt's call for help and waited." Her gaze clashed with his. "She would've had to act fast, which means she was close by. I need to call the sheriff. She's hiding in plain sight."

"There are a lot of cabins on the mountain. She could be in any one of them." He sat across from her. "It would take days…weeks…to find the right one."

"The sooner they start looking, the better." She grabbed her phone from the coffee table and called Sheriff Westbrook.

He listened quietly while she explained her theory. "We'll see about getting a chopper in the air. It would help if we knew what vehicle she drove. Has O'Connor shown up yet? I want him there to help guard the place."

"If he's here, he hasn't let us know." She relayed the question to Zeke who peered out the window.

"He's outside on his phone."

"He's here," Shea said.

"Good. Take it easy, Deputy." He hung up.

A few seconds later, footsteps sounded on the porch outside. Zeke opened the door to let Graham in.

The other deputy's gaze fell on Shea. "You doing okay?"

"Yes. Thank you for preventing Amber from getting to me in the hospital."

He grinned. "Just doing my job." He set a duffel bag on the floor. "I hope you have a spare room, Zeke. My orders are to stay with the two of you until this woman is caught."

"This place has lots of rooms." Zeke grabbed the bag. "I'll put you in the first room on the right. Anyone trying to get to Shea has to go through you then me."

The fact everyone seemed to think Shea helpless

rankled. "My gun hand is still functional. I don't need to be babied."

Both men stared at her then at each other before heading down the hall. Great. Not only were they treating her like a baby, now they treated her like a hysterical female spouting nonsense. At least that's how her father acted when her mother said anything he didn't understand or agree with.

She gave a half sigh, half groan, and lay back on the sofa pillows. She'd lay low for three days. That was it. Three days of rest and poring over case files. Then, she'd be out there questioning folks with a vengeance. Someone knew something.

Her parents' original neighbors no longer lived in the neighborhood, so going back there would be a waste of time. Any statements they'd made were in the files. Shea could find out where those neighbors lived now and pay them a visit or make a phone call.

While she lay there, her mind raced with possible ways to seek justice for her father's murder. Finally get closure. Find out who was behind Amber trying to kill Shea, then hunt that person down and put them behind bars.

She fell asleep and woke to Zeke and Graham speaking in low voices from the dining room table.

"So, these are all about her father's murder?" Graham asked.

"As far as I know," Zeke responded. "I'd like to help her solve this."

They were going through her father's files? Shea hadn't given them permission. Those were hers!

She sat up so fast her head spun and fire shot through the upper portion of her arm. She waited until she steadied, then marched toward the men the best she could. "I did not say you could go through those."

Zeke gave a determined look. "You left the box on the table. Let us help you. We might see something you missed."

"No. Put those back." She hitched her chin. "You had no right."

"Actually, I did. It's my house. Someone is trying to kill my houseguest. I need to know what you brought in here."

Anger fueled her words. "If that's how you feel, then I'll move back to the rental. I have a guest room for Graham. You can rattle around in this big house all by yourself." She headed for her room.

"Don't be ridiculous." He rushed after her, slowly turning her to face him. "I'm sorry. That was a rotten thing to say. I'm trying to help you. Let us help you." His gaze implored her. "You could've been killed, Shea. Let's work together to find this person."

She studied the face that had grown so dear to her. "Fine, but next time ask first. You're right, though. Three heads are definitely better than one."

~

Amber waited, hunched down and shivering among the grapevines. Clouds obscured the moon, leaving the area covered in shadows. All she needed now was for them in the house to go to sleep.

She'd use the key in her pocket to enter the back door, then she'd find out which room the woman deputy slept in. The soft-soled shoes she wore wouldn't make a sound on Zeke's wooden floors. She'd be in and out before the woman could open her eyes and see the face of her killer.

Zeke would definitely have nothing to do with Amber once she'd committed the act, but she was no longer sure she wanted him anyway. All he'd done in the cabin before stealing her gun was lie. No woman wanted a liar.

Not turning down ten thousand dollars had been a no-brainer. It wouldn't make her rich, but it would get her to Mexico. She hated snow. She'd head to a tropical place, open a beachside bar, maybe…the lights in the house flickered off.

Finally. Now, to wait until they all fell asleep. She blew on her frigid fingers. Fifteen minutes, then she'd go in.

Fifteen minutes later, her fingers frozen chunks of flesh, she pulled the key from her pocket and advanced toward the house.

~

Zeke couldn't sleep. Not with worrying about Shea. Maybe he could talk her into going away for a while. He could take her to Europe. No one would find her there.

No, she had a job to do. Not just the deputy job, but finding out who killed her father. She'd never leave.

He sat up and slid his feet into slippers. He'd bought a pie a few days ago. Hopefully, a slice would make him drowsy.

A shadowy form stopped in his doorway then continued past. Most likely Graham making the rounds before heading to bed for himself. Wait. No.

He stepped into the hall. The person entered Shea's room.

"Everyone up! Intruder in Shea's room." Zeke grabbed a golf club he'd set by the door and hurried forward.

A shot rang out.

Glass shattered.

A woman shrieked.

Zeke darted into the room, Graham on his heels, to see Amber climbing out the window, Shea sitting in her bed clutching a gun.

"Don't just stand there. Go after her." She motioned the gun at the window. "I only nicked her. Stupid hand wasn't steady."

Zeke jumped through the window, rolling through the snow. He shoved aside the fact he wore nothing but pajama bottoms and slippers and searched the area for a glimpse of Amber.

Graham glanced at the club in his hand. "Don't you own a gun?"

"It's locked up. I only use it for hunting. You go that way, I'll go this way. She's probably in the vineyard." Which covered a lot of ground.

"Okay, but you need to carry a gun until this is over."

Zeke frowned and peered around the corner of the house. Footsteps in the snow led from the vineyard to the house and back the other way. She had fled into the field.

Staying low, he caught the deputy's attention, then pointed. "I'm going back to Shea. I don't want her alone."

"I'll go after the intruder."

Zeke nodded and darted back to the house. Shea sat up in bed, her bedside lamp on.

"You okay?" He asked.

"Thanks to you. I'd taken a pill and would never have woken up without your yell." She eyed the club in his hand. "That against a gun?"

"Enough. I'll start carrying until this is over." He sat in the chair next to the window. Drops of blood lingered on the sill. "How bad did you hit her?"

"The way she dashed through that window so fast means not badly. What I'm hoping at this point is that it's enough to make her go away until I'm stronger." She lay back against the pillows. "Then, let her come."

If someone would've told him a year ago Amber would turn into an assassin, he'd have laughed. Pretty, petite Amber turned into a killer?

He stood and went to the room at the end of the hall where he could look out into the field. His eyes strained to see through the dark.

She joined him, a robe pulled over one shoulder. "Anything?"

He reached over and draped the other end over her other shoulder. "No. I can't see Graham or Amber. It's too dark."

They watched for close to half an hour before the clouds parted to reveal Graham exiting the field. He glanced up at the window and gave them a thumbs-down.

Zeke helped Shea down the stairs, and they met him in the living room. "Well?"

"She's bleeding pretty good. I followed the drops for as long as I could. She exited the vineyard and went into the woods. Too dark to see anything in there." Graham plopped into a chair by the fireplace. "Can we light one? I'm an icicle."

Zeke picked up a remote that turned on the fireplace. "It's gas."

"I don't care as long as it's warm." The deputy pushed to his feet and stood in front of the flame. "I'll have to call this into the sheriff. It bothers me she got past both of us to reach Shea. That's skill."

The thought scared Zeke half out of his mind. "She got past the security system, too. I'll call the company and get it changed immediately."

Shea rolled her eyes. "You didn't change it after the two of you broke up?"

"Didn't think I needed to." What an idiot he was. Definitely too trusting. He'd learned a very valuable lesson. One that could've gotten Shea killed. "What do we do now?"

"Fix the security issue."

"I'll call the security company as soon as they open. I'll also buy a couple of big dogs."

"The world's best warning system." Graham rolled his shoulders. "Plus, they could've chased her down. Try and get some sleep. I'll sit up for the next few hours."

Zeke helped Shea to her room then moved through every room of the house to peek out the windows. Was she there watching, or had she gone into hiding to lick her wounds?

Chapter Fifteen

She'd kill him someday. Just as soon as she found out his identity. Amber groaned and pulled up the hem of her shirt. The deputy's bullet seemed to have passed through. She'd left a lot of blood behind, but nothing that time wouldn't replenish.

Amber researched online how to stitch up a wound, poured disinfectant over the hole, and then screamed as fire ripped through her. She'd told the man who'd hired her that she'd been shot and needed help. Did he care? No. Said hurry up and get better and finish the job, or he'd find someone who could.

Now, she hid in a cheap motel that rented rooms by the hour so she could heal. Oh, yes, she'd take great pleasure killing the man who had hired her.

After cleaning, stitching, and bandaging her wound, she lay on the bed and stared at a water mark on the ceiling that looked a bit like the state of Texas. Zeke would change his security code so getting inside his house would be almost impossible. If she was to kill the deputy, she'd have to do so while the woman was outside or in town.

Since she was also recuperating from bullet wounds, she wouldn't be in town for a few days. Fine with

Amber. She closed her eyes to get some much-needed rest.

~

Zeke made three omelets and carried them to the table where Shea and Graham dug through the cold-case files. "Any luck?"

"Still looks as if it has something to do with Buford." Shea shook her head. "After his concern the other night, I have a hard time believing he'd have hired anyone."

"Then, it has to be someone close to him." Zeke set the plates down. "David Real would've been the closest, but as mayor, my uncle was surrounded by people all the time. Who would've benefited most from your father's death?"

"Someone with secrets." Graham cut into his omelet. "What kind of a politician was your uncle?"

"A good one." Buford stepped into the room. "What's going on here, and why am I the topic of conversation?"

"Omelet?" Zeke held out his plate.

"Sure." Buford sat and dug in. "Well?"

Zeke cracked more eggs into a bowl as Shea explained her reason for coming to Misty Hollow and Graham's thoughts. He expected his uncle to explode, but instead, he remained silent, which made Zeke study him over his shoulder.

Buford ate, his brow furrowed. When he'd eaten every bit of the omelet, he straightened. "By good, I meant deceitful. I took money under the table as payment for some dubious things. David Real was right in the thick with me. If your father suspected something wasn't right, he'd have gone to David before me."

Zeke slid his omelet onto a plate and joined the others at the table. "We were in Real's office. He's the one we told the lie to about being engaged."

"He's the one who told me you two were getting hitched. Then, I saw your ex at the store and told her. See what lies will get you?" He shrugged. "Anyway, my money is on David as to the one who killed your old man. As God is my witness, I had nothing to do with his death. I might be a lot of things, but a murderer isn't one of them."

"Okay." Shea pushed half her omelet away. "What is the best way to approach Real?"

"I'll give him a call. Tell him to meet me at the bar like old times. Then, you can swoop in and start asking questions."

"The same woman who shot Shea tried again last night." Zeke glanced from Buford to Shea. "This time, Shea shot her, but she still escaped. I'm changing the security code and getting a couple of watchdogs."

"Good idea. I know a man who trains dogs." Buford pulled his phone from his pocket and made the call. "Doesn't matter what breed as long as they're fierce." He hung up. "You'll have your dogs before noon. What else do you want me to do?"

"Why the change in your behavior?" Shea's glare pierced his. "You've gone from surly to wanting to help."

Zeke had wondered the same thing but knew getting too personal with his uncle usually didn't end well.

"The other night opened my eyes. Other than Sybil, Zeke is the only family I have. I could've lost him. Why? Because I lost my temper with my wife enough that she called him to come help her." His shoulders sagged. "It's time to seek help to control my anger and my drinking. Life is too short."

"That's the best news I've heard in a very long time." Zeke grinned, his heart hopeful. "It's good to have the real Buford back." It had been a long time coming.

When Zeke had been young, he'd spent a lot of time with Buck and Buford, tagging along with them as if they were two more fathers. Then, when his father died, he'd spent even more time with Buford until he started drinking while running for mayor. Liquid courage, he'd said.

"No mushy talk. Just stay out of the clutches of that woman." He planted his hands flat on the table and pushed to his feet. "I'm headed to rehab, but I wanted to stop by here first. I'll be gone for twenty-eight days. Keep an eye on your aunt for me. As for Real, let me know. I'll find a way to get phone calls." Without another word, he turned and left the house.

"What a transformation." Shea's wide-eyed stare followed Buford through the window. "I think he actually loves you."

"Here's hoping he doesn't revert back." Zeke had seen his uncle try and change before. Hopefully, this time he'd be successful.

Tires crunched outside. Graham motioned for Zeke and Shea to remain seated while he checked on who the visitor was. "Okay. It's a man with two big dogs."

Zeke held out his hand to Shea. She slipped hers in his, and he helped her to her feet. Keeping her hand in his, he led her to the front porch where two of the biggest dogs he'd ever seen jumped from the back of a battered pickup truck.

"Meet Beast and Tank. Mixed breed." A heavyset

man in denim overalls ambled toward them. "They don't bark at just anything, so if they are barking, something or someone is out there. You want them to attack? All you need to do is say, 'Get 'em.'"

Both dogs glanced up at him.

"And wave your hand. See how they're waiting? Down, boys. Two hundred dollars apiece if you want them. Both two years old."

Shea glanced at Zeke. "Buy them."

He couldn't refuse her anything. Even two ugly mutts. "I'll write a check."

~

Shea approached the dogs as Zeke went in the house.

"Hold up." Graham shot out a hand to stop her. "You don't know how they'll respond to you."

"Come here," the man in the overalls ordered. "Give me your hand."

Shea held out her hand.

He took it and lay it on one dog's head, then the other before stepping back. "They now know they are yours."

"But..." She glanced toward the house. "They're supposed to be Zeke's."

"So, hand 'em over. Makes no difference to me. I found these mutts on the side of the road and trained 'em. They aren't my pets."

The two dogs immediately sat one on each side of Shea. She smiled, feeling safer than she'd ever felt before. The two made formidable bookends.

Zeke returned, check in hand, and glanced at the dogs. "Made friends already?"

"Since you other two men were here when I dropped

them off, they'll consider you part of the pack. If anyone else comes, I'd suggest they stay in their vehicle until you tell the dogs it's okay." He pocketed the check and climbed in his truck where he rolled down the window. "Off your property, they're friendly enough unless you give them the signal. Enjoy."

"I had no idea dogs came with so many instructions." Shea patted the one on her right then peered at the tag on his collar. "The brown one is Beast. That makes you—" she patted the black one's head, "Tank. Are you hungry?" They'd cost a fortune in dog food.

Two tails thumped the ground.

"Let's move 'em inside." Zeke glanced at the sky. "Looks like rain."

"Better than snow." Shea headed for the house, the two dogs following.

Inside, they both lay between her and the door. Maybe she should've adopted a dog a long time ago. She curled up on the sofa and prepared for a long day of watching TV. "Are you going to have Buford call David Real?"

Zeke shook his head. "Not unless you want to wait almost a month. Buford won't be released for any bar dates. It's not a good idea for him to meet in a bar when he gets out. Too much temptation. We'll have to come up with an idea of our own."

"If we had Amber's contact information, we could give her a call and ask her to lure Real out." Shea chuckled. "Set the two against each other." If Real was the man she searched for.

Had her father discovered Buford took bribes? Had Real gotten a cut of the money in order to keep his mouth shut? Was it enough to cause him to kill her father sniper-style? Her mind whirled with questions. She stiffened. "How did Real find Amber? He had to have gotten her phone number somehow. If he did, then we can too."

"I'll get right on it." Graham pulled a laptop from a computer bag and set it on the coffee table. His fingers flew over the keys. "This her?" He turned the computer around so Zeke could see. "I saw her in the supermarket but only caught a glimpse."

"That's her."

"How long has she lived in Misty Hollow?"

"About four years."

Graham nodded. "I'll call our one and only cell phone store. We might get lucky. You sure you don't have her number?"

"I deleted it right after I fired her, but I could look in the office. It's probably in her file." He palmed his forehead. "Unless I shredded it."

"Why would you do that?" Shea frowned.

"Because I was mad." He rushed to the office.

Mad? She didn't think Zeke got mad. At least not mad enough to shred information on an employee.

He returned a few minutes later with an manila folder. "I guess I only shredded the love letters." He handed Graham the folder. "Address, phone—it's all here."

"You figure out what you want to say then give her a call. I'll contact the landlord to this apartment complex and see whether she still lives there." Graham grabbed his phone from the table. "Then, I'll work on tracking Real down. If he gets word we're on to him, he'll run."

"How do you call the person who abducted you and

tried to kill your houseguest to ask about Real?" Shea plucked at the fringe on a crocheted afghan that looked as if it had seen better days. "Who made this?"

"My grandmother." He smiled. "Can't bear to get rid of it."

"I wouldn't either." She felt restless. The two men had a task to focus on. Here she sat, one arm in a sling, with nothing to do.

Beast lay his massive head on her leg. She idly played with his ears. "I guess we need to get you some food."

Zeke glanced up. "I'll order a delivery. We'll buy food, dishes, and beds."

"I'll pay you back." Since the dogs seemed to have claimed her, it was only right.

"No need. I've always wanted a couple of dogs around the place." He made the call. "What we need to be thinking about is what to say to Amber."

Chapter Sixteen

"**Why not ask** her straight out why she wants to kill me?" Shea pulled the afghan up to her chin. "She seems straightforward enough. It's not exactly a secret."

Zeke rubbed his chin. "Doesn't hurt to try, I guess." He glanced at Graham.

"Go ahead. She hasn't been back to her apartment since the supermarket incident. Maybe you can flush her out." He tapped his forefinger on the papers in front of him. "David Real was in Little Rock on the night of your father's shooting. He'd attended a play, had dinner, and seemingly retired to his room. At least that's what the papers say. My question is…why was he questioned in the first place? He had no ties to your father. Matchett was here in Misty Hollow. Fill that hole and you might have proof on Real. Hold on." He typed some more, read some, then glanced up with a grin. "Real was a sharpshooter in the army. Only did four years, but he has the skill to play sniper."

Things were looking more and more like Real killed her father. If she hadn't been so fixated on Buford, she might have discovered it herself. Maybe she wasn't cut out to be law enforcement. Good law enforcement officers could remain neutral and follow the facts not emotions.

"My father could have discovered Real was getting a cut of the bribe money. Real went to Little Rock for a night on the town—"

"A convention, actually," Graham said. "A headhunter's convention."

"We could question some of the attendees about whether or not Real actually went to his room. Maybe someone saw him sneak out." Hope leaped in her. "Someone might remember details even after ten years."

Graham nodded. "I'll come up with a list."

"I'm calling Amber. Everyone stay quiet. I'll put her on speaker." Zeke punched in the number from a sheet of paper.

"Wow." Amber coughed. "I can't believe you still have my number. That actually touches my heart."

Shea rolled her eyes and laid her head back on the sofa pillows.

"Do you have a minute?" Zeke carefully placed the phone on the coffee table.

"For you, always."

Shea wanted to gag.

Zeke took a deep breath. "Why are you trying to kill Deputy Sydney? After you abducted me and I escaped, why didn't you run?"

"Oh, Zeke. Why do you care? You said the two of you weren't an item."

"We're not." His gaze locked with Shea's.

She huffed. "It's nothing personal with the deputy. I'm simply being paid a good sum of money to get rid of her. Being a hit person pays so much more than being your sommelier did. I may continue in the future."

"Are you being paid by David Real?"

Graham rapidly shook his head. His shoulders sagged.

Zeke mouthed, "Sorry."

"Is that his name? I had no idea who I was working with." Her breath shuddered. "Thank you for letting me know."

"How badly injured are you?"

"How sweet. I'll survive. Tell the deputy I'll be in touch in a few days." Click.

"Man." Graham shot to his feet and paced. "She'll alert Real now."

"I blurted out. All this law-and-order stuff is new to me." He took Shea's hand. "She isn't going to stop."

"Not until we stop her." Shea needed to heal quickly. Even with the two dogs, Amber could reach her. She'd simply pick her off like she tried to at Buford's. The next time, she might be a better shot. "Put a trace on her phone."

"Already in progress," Graham said, shooting Zeke a look of frustration before shaking his head and returning to the table.

Tires crunched outside.

Graham sprang to his feet and peered through the peephole. "Pet delivery. I'll get it."

"I'll help. We're safe enough until Amber is on her feet. I could tell she was hurting."

Shea waited, helpless, while the men carried in the things for the dogs. Both dogs remained by her side while their focus never left the front door. They stayed poised to follow her order if she gave it.

A few minutes later, two dog beds sat in Shea's room and their dishes in the kitchen. The rental wouldn't have room for such beasts. They'd have to remain here with Zeke until this was all over. It was for the best. She worked a lot of hours as a deputy.

Shea tossed aside the afghan and pushed to her feet. The least she could do was make sandwiches for lunch. Idleness would kill her faster than a bullet.

"What are you doing?" Zeke paused, a large bag of dog food over one shoulder.

"Fixing lunch for us."

"With one arm?" He arched a brow.

"Yes." She'd manage. "I have to do something."

In the kitchen, she stared into a sparse but large walk-in pantry. Zeke really needed to start eating better. She grabbed a half a loaf of bread, some canned chicken, and then moved to the fridge. A jar of mayo and some cheddar cheese. She'd make chicken salad sandwiches. "Since I have to stay here for an indefinite amount of time, I'm making a grocery list."

"Anything you need." Zeke set the dog food in the pantry. "If you feel up to it later, considering you refuse to rest, I'd like to show you the winery."

"I'd like that." Anything to relieve the boredom looming over her head. Now that they'd figured out the most likely person to have killed her father, she no longer needed to pore over the case. All that was left was to heal and confront David Real.

~

"I do hope you have somewhere to go, Mr. Real," Amber said.

"How do you know my name?" David froze.

"Zeke Matchett. Seems they're on to you. I want half the money now or I turn you in. The second half can be paid when the job is done."

"You'll finish the task?" His grip tightened on his

phone.

"If you pay me the half, I will. I have plans for that money, Mr. Real. Plans on getting the heck out of Misty Hollow. The country, even. I suggest you make plans of your own."

He glanced around the office of the business he'd grown from the ground up. It was just a job not his passion. "Where should I leave the check?"

"Not a check. It's only a matter of time before your account is closed. Cash. There's a bench at the lake with a small plaque that says, 'In loving memory of Danny.' Leave the cash there at four p.m. I'll be watching. There will be a burner phone. Destroy the phone you have now. I'll call you so you know the number of my new phone."

"You want me to go out in the rain?"

"Less likely to encounter people. If you aren't there, I make a call to the sheriff." She hung up. Time for David to realize who was actually calling the shots.

~

The sheriff entered the house but froze at the sight of the two growling dogs.

"It's okay," Shea said, putting a hand on Tank's head. "He's a friend."

"Got them this morning." Zeke thrust out his hand. "What brings you out on this rainy afternoon?"

Still eyeing the dogs, Sheriff Westbrook said, "Graham sent me an email that you believe David Real is the man hiring Miss Solely. I went by his place of business. The office was locked up tight, so I called the receptionist. She said Real closed the place down with no word of explanation and sent her home. I went to his house. The front door had been left unlocked. It's clear he left in a hurry. So, I headed to the bank. Sure enough, he withdrew two hundred thousand dollars." He shook his head. "The bank manager wasn't happy."

"Does he have money left in his account?" Zeke stepped back. "Hey, would you like a cup of coffee? Take off that wet coat?"

"A lot of money. We're trying to close the account so he can't get to it anymore." The sheriff shrugged out of his coat, droplets falling to the wooden floor. "A cup of hot coffee sounds wonderful."

Zeke hung the coat on a rack near the door. "Guess Graham told you I let it slip that we thought the culprit was Real." He headed for the kitchen.

"He did. Accidents happen." His eyes fell on the box on the table. "Case file on Shea's father?"

"Yes. We don't need it strewn across the table anymore."

"Stay." Shea ordered the dogs to remain in the living room and joined Zeke and the sheriff in the kitchen. She'd somehow managed to change into a button-up shirt for the tour of the winery. "Amber is going to continue with her assignment to kill me." She sat in a kitchen chair. "Doesn't make sense now that we know who I came to Misty Hollow for, but there it is."

"She did say she liked her new job." Zeke poured the sheriff a cup of coffee. "The gal obviously has some mental issues."

"That's obvious." Shea handed him a grocery list. "For when you have time."

"I'll place the order after the tour." He pocketed the paper after groaning at the list of vegetables and healthy meats. "What's the next move, Sheriff?"

"I've people scouring the area for signs of either of them. We're checking motels and vacant buildings, although I don't expect to find them in a vacant warehouse or house. It's too cold." He accepted the cup Zeke handed him. "Thanks."

"I want to come back to work next week." Shea lifted her chin.

"Not until this is over." The sheriff faced her. "While you can do your job with one hand, you can't get into an altercation. You'd be at a huge disadvantage." He arched a brow. "Unless you'd be happy with desk work?"

"No." She scowled. "If I had use of both my arms, I'd cross them right now."

Zeke laughed. "Come on. Let's take that tour. Thanks for coming by and letting us know about Real, Sheriff."

Shea called for the dogs to follow. Zeke led her through a door of the house that entered the room full of barrels of wine. "This is where we age the wine. I'm working on some new variations with different grapes." Which had fallen to the wayside under current circumstances.

"Have you always wanted to run the vineyard?"

"Never really thought about it. It was expected of me, so it's a good thing I have the knack." He ran a hand over the barrel. "I guess these are like my babies."

"Do you want kids someday?" She asked softly.

"Yeah. With the right woman." His gaze focused on her lips. Soft and full. He wanted to kiss her very much.

She must have read his mind because her eyes widened, and she stepped back. "Uh, how long until these are ready to be bottled?"

"Some will be ready come spring." He led her through another door. "Fermentation room." Large stainless-steel vats filled the room.

"A person could get drunk just breathing the air in here."

He laughed and opened another door. "Here's where the tasting takes place. I've closed it down for the worst part of winter. I'll open back up in a few weeks."

He watched as her gaze roamed the polished counter and aisles of bottles of wine.

"This is a beautiful place."

"Come here." He took her hand and led her to a large window.

Her lips parted, and she gasped. "Oh, Zeke."

He tore his gaze away from her enraptured face and looked out the window. The valley of Misty Hollow lay under a slowing rain. "You should see it when everything is green. That view alone is why my grandfather built this place in this very spot."

A cool breeze wafted his way. He turned as the dogs, noses to the ground, headed through the door to the stockroom. Leaving Shea to continue enjoying the view, he followed.

The lock on the door where deliveries were dropped off had been broken, the knob removed. The cold winter wind blew through the hole. Someone must have planned on entering this way. Did they, and if so, where were they?

Chapter Seventeen

Zeke called Graham to come to the winery. While he and Shea waited, he poured her a small glass of his best wine. Would they ever have a day they could spend like normal people?

She took a sip and set the glass on the counter. "Do you have anything sweeter?"

"With carbonation?" He arched a brow.

"That sounds good, but mostly just sweeter. I'm not a fan of the dry wines." She glanced in the direction of the large window. Her shoulders sagged, then she returned her attention to Zeke. "Still raining."

He appreciated her attempt to act as if nothing was wrong. "Don't worry. No sniper bullet can come this far." Not with the nearest ridge miles away.

"I wasn't worried." She accepted the next glass of wine to taste and took a sip. "Much better." She motioned for him to add more. "You ought to open shop. Wine tasting is something people would brave the weather for. Especially if you offered food, at least a charcuterie board."

"That's a good idea." One he'd considered, but with all that had happened over the last few weeks, letting strangers into his winery didn't sound wise.

Graham entered the winery. "Got a break-in?"

"It seems that way, although there's no other sign that anyone entered. Just a broken lock. Do you think they planned on coming back?" Zeke followed the deputy into the storeroom.

He processed the scene. "That's a good guess. How's she holding up?" He jerked his head toward the wine-tasting room.

"A bit quiet today. Shea can't seem to get out of her head. She came to Misty Hollow with a strong belief only to find out she was wrong. That's a big life change."

"Well, she's living under your roof. You know her better than anyone. Find out what's going on. We're going to need her in order to catch these guys." Graham's brow furrowed. "She needs a strong mind, Zeke."

"I know. I'll figure something out." He headed back to the counter. "Another one?"

Shea gave a sad smile. "Funny how sound carries in such a big place, isn't it?" She waved her hand to say no to more wine.

"Sorry. We're just worried about you." He reached for her hand only to have her pull away.

"I'm tired. Think I'll take a nap." She slid from the stool and exited through the door that would lead her back to the main house. The two dogs glanced his way as if waiting for him to join her. When he didn't, they followed Shea.

He took his time cleaning the few items they'd used, knowing she could reach her room without him. He'd give her time. After ten minutes had passed, he returned to the house and closeted himself in his office.

Zeke did want to reopen the winery all year, but he couldn't do it all himself. He'd need another sommelier, staff for the charcuterie boards, someone to wait the counter…he started making a list. Anything to feel as if he lived a normal day without some crazy person out there with a gun.

~

Amber shivered until her teeth chattered. She ran a fever which made the cold worse. Why couldn't the idiot be early? She popped some fever relief and swallowed them dry. She'd need some serious first aid when she returned to the room. With the police searching everywhere, Amber had to keep changing locations. This afternoon, she'd gone back to the first place she'd stayed since the sheriff's men had already gone there.

A waterdrop fell off the tree branch over her head, sending an icy droplet down her collar. Amber cursed the weather, her wound, and Real.

She should have pushed for the whole amount. If he wanted his dirty work done bad enough, he'd pay up. Perhaps she'd use her gun to make him pay. Her mind raced with all she could do with the money.

Living in Mexico would mean a lower cost of living. Then she'd have enough money to travel the world as a great assassin. She'd make more money than she could imagine.

Amber blew on her hands to warm them. She'd have to buy a bulletproof vest, though. She really hated getting shot.

Finally. A tall, skinny, balding man moved into sight. He carried a navy duffel bag.

Amber studied the area. He appeared to be alone. Of course, he was. To alert the authorities about Amber, he'd also expose himself. She felt confident enough to step out of hiding.

"Mr. Real." She reached for the bag.

"Miss Solely. Did you find a way in?"

"I've already been in the house, sir. That's how I got shot."

"Then how are you going to finish this?"

"It'll be done." She pulled her gun from her pocket and aimed it at his head. "This is what's going to happen. You're going to go back to whatever hole you're hiding in and write me a letter of reference. I plan on making this a career, so write a good one. You're also going to return here in exactly one hour with the rest of my money, or I kill you before I off the sheriff. Your time starts now."

He opened his mouth to protest then muttered something under his breath before skittering away.

She wasn't completely positive, but she thought he said something about having been a sniper in the army. So what? Amber didn't fear his threats.

~

What Zeke and Graham had said shouldn't have bothered her that much. After all, it was all true.

Shea lay in bed for an hour staring at the ceiling. The snores from the dogs made her smile on occasion. Although she didn't nap, she did rest and felt better for doing so. She sat up and slid her feet into slippers.

The two dogs were immediately alert and followed her to the kitchen where the aroma of baked bread greeted Shea. "You baked bread?"

Zeke laughed. "Graham did. I can pretty much only make eggs. Which is why I order out a lot."

She shot the other deputy a quick glance. "It looks gorgeous."

"I used to bake with my grandmother all the time.

Even won a few awards." He grinned and crossed his arms. "The actual cooking has to rest on someone else's shoulder."

"I can cook. Were the groceries delivered?"

"Yes." Zeke opened the pantry to show her the full shelves. "You tell me what to do. I'll follow your instructions to the letter."

"I'll make it easy on you. We'll do spaghetti, a salad, and some slices of Graham's bread with garlic butter." She perched on a stool. "Fill a big pot with water. Are you helping, Graham?"

"Nope. I already contributed. There's a ball game on I intend to watch." He moved to the living room.

Zeke apparently knew the basics about making spaghetti. He plopped salad fixings, some minced garlic, and a stick of butter in front of Shea. "What goes in the pasta sauce?"

"You don't want it from a jar?" She raised her eyebrows but told him the ingredients.

He mixed them a bit at a time until he achieved the taste he wanted.

Shea smiled and did her best to cut vegetables with one hand.

"Sorry. Use this thing." He handed her a slicer.

"This would have been useful fifteen minutes ago." She glanced at the mostly torn rather than chopped lettuce. She handed Zeke the mushrooms and grated the carrots. "I'm sorry."

"For what?" He paused the slicing.

"My reaction earlier. I know you care." She dropped the carrot shavings into the bowl of lettuce. "I became a deputy because of my father's death and my quest for revenge. I moved to Misty Hollow because of the same.

Now, my entire last ten years don't matter. What if I hadn't become a deputy? What would I have done with my life?"

"Do you like being a deputy?"

"I don't know." It pained her to say that. She was good at her job, but was she passionate about it? "To be honest, I'm feeling a bit aimless."

"Being stuck inside because of injuries and bad weather doesn't help. That's why I suggested the winery tour." He finished the mushrooms and moved to the radishes.

"Water's boiling over."

"Ah." He whirled and lifted the pot off the stove. When the bubbles subsided a bit, he broke spaghetti noodles in half and dropped them in. "Graham's worried about you doing your job."

"Oh, I'll do it as long as it's mine to do."

"You might quit?" His mouth dropped open.

She shrugged. "I really haven't decided. I don't think making that decision close to being shot is a good time. When I'm healed and Amber and Real are behind bars, then I'll make a decision." She glanced toward the living room. "Don't tell Graham, okay?"

"Not a word." He stirred the spaghetti then started mixing the butter and garlic.

It was sloppy, but Shea managed to butter the bread. "These should be toasted by the time the spaghetti is done. Don't forget they're in the oven."

"What do you think you're sitting there for?" He grinned and slid the pan into the oven. "Now that the sheriff knows your reason for moving here, he won't be blindsided if you quit."

If being the big word. Only time would tell whether

she was meant to remain a deputy. She'd wait.

Zeke's sauce turned out to be fabulous. "I wish you'd written down how much you put in of each thing. I want to keep this."

"I'll make it anytime you ask." His warm gaze heated her face.

The man in front of her was another reason she couldn't decide on her future. She'd never met anyone like him before, and her feelings for him had long since gone past friendship. The last thing Zeke needed was a flake. Someone who didn't know what they wanted to be when they grew up.

She turned to Graham. "How long will the sheriff have you here?"

"Until you're able to use both arms, I reckon." He patted his stomach. "The three of us make a good meal."

The sheriff obviously didn't see a long-term reason for a guard. Probably because of the dogs. That suited her fine because once she could use both arms, she planned on a face-to-face with Amber. Something the sheriff wouldn't like. Not if he knew her plan to lure the woman out.

Shea's first plan had set in motion something that shouldn't have been. Her next plan might send the woman further over the edge. She picked up her plate and carried it to the sink. Zeke wouldn't like the plan either, but she might be able to carry it out without him knowing.

After she loaded the dishwasher, she joined the men in the living room. Not interested in the football game, she flipped through her phone, reading news and watching videos. Not a word about Amber and only a small mention that David Real was missing. More confirmation that Shea would have to do something to bring this all closer to fruition.

Beast lifted his head. An ear twitched. Both dogs jumped to their feet and ran to the back door, growling.

She gave chase, the men right after her.

Through the window, an orange glow lit up the sky. "The rental's on fire."

"The grapevines." Zeke yanked open the door and sprinted outside.

Chapter Eighteen

Shea removed her sling and sprinted after Zeke. She couldn't help fight a fire with one arm. If the vines burned, Zeke would lose everything.

Graham quickly passed her, his arms full of blankets. "Where's the closest water source?"

"I've a hose and spigot every third of the field." Zeke grabbed a blanket and dashed to the edge of his property. "Too late to save Shea's house."

Everything she had other than what could fit in a duffel bag was in that house. Not that it had ever been a home—she hadn't lived there long enough—but her clothes and books…

Shaking off the sadness, she grabbed a blanket and soaked it at the nearest faucet. The stitches in her shoulder pulled and burned as she slapped the wet blanket at the flames inching toward the sleeping grapevines.

"Stop." Zeke cast a sharp glance her way. "You shouldn't be working that arm."

"I'll heal. It doesn't hurt that much." Shea beat at a bush that had caught fire. She'd lied. Every motion tore at her stitches.

Flames licked the night sky to her left. "Another

fire!" She dashed that way.

"Over here, too." Graham raced in the other direction.

Someone wanted to trap them in the field. Shea glanced toward the house, their only avenue of escape.

Beast and Tank stared in that direction and barked, their hackles raised.

A tall, thin man dressed all in black ran past with a torch. He touched the torch to every shrub he passed.

Fear choked Shea. Smoke blurred her vision. "It's Real." There was no way they could fight off a fire of this magnitude. "He's trapped us."

"Pray those clouds overhead drop their rain soon," Zeke said, "or we're all goners." Soot marred his handsome face. "We'll keep fighting the flames. Hopefully, we can keep ourselves alive and save most of the vines before help comes."

She didn't share his hope but continued battling the flames until lifting the wet blanket became virtually impossible. She leaned against the faucet and watched as the inferno threatened Zeke's livelihood. If the fire succeeded in destroying the vineyard it would take years to recover.

"The fire seems to be staying along the perimeter." Graham joined her. "With all the snow we've had, the ground is pretty damp."

"So, it's to keep us out here to freeze?" Not likely. All they had to do was stand close enough to the fire to stay warm. "Maybe Real doesn't mean to kill us."

"He burned down the house you'd rented." Zeke shook his head. "I think lighting the perimeter was an afterthought when he realized you didn't burn with the house."

"Why keep on trying to get rid of me? The harm is done. The sheriff knows he's the guilty person. Why didn't he pick us off when we came out of the house? He was a sharpshooter in the army." Shea wet her blanket again now that she'd had a few minutes' rest and started beating at the flames again. "Tell me someone called the fire department."

"I did." Graham started beating the flames, too, as a spark blew in and ignited one of the vines.

A few minutes later, the wind picked up. Zeke's shoulders sagged. "Let's beat a way out of here. We can't save the vines now. The fire will spread rapidly."

A raindrop landed on Shea's nose. "I never took you for a quitter. It's starting to rain. We can hold off the fire until then." She squeezed his hand. "We're going to be cold and wet soon. Let's get busy."

He studied her face for a minute then nodded. "You're right. Don't quit as long as there is a flicker of success."

Was David Real still paying Amber to kill her, or had the two parted ways? Had Shea injured Amber too severely for her to continue? She slapped the blanket against the ground. Shea might have been lucky so far not to be killed, but she wasn't lucky enough for Amber to be out of the picture.

The rain fell harder. A firetruck, lights flashing, pulled up to the grapevines. Within minutes, they had cleared a path for them to escape.

She slipped her hand into Zeke's. "We did it."

"With a little help from above." He smiled, his teeth flashing white in a face covered with soot. "Thank you."

"You're welcome." In the house, she headed for the guest bathroom and showered then gingerly put her arm back in its sling. Luckily, she hadn't torn any stitches, but the wound throbbed. She returned to the kitchen and stared out the window as Zeke spoke with one of the firemen.

His face was free of soot, and he'd changed clothes. Good. All Shea wanted now was her warm bed.

~

That was fun. David laughed as he sped to the neighboring town he'd decided to hole up in for a while.

His original plan had been to burn the deputy in her house. Amber had neglected to tell him the woman lived under Matchett's roof. Nor had he known about the other deputy. Security was tight around the vineyard. The dogs had been another surprise. Or had Amber told him?

He shrugged. It didn't matter. Getting to Deputy Sydney would be a lot harder than before. He should've killed her the same way he had her father. He didn't have time to play games.

Since Amber had demanded full payment, he needed the job done before she tried getting even more money from him. He wasn't a bank!

Who would've guessed such a pretty lady could have such a cold heart? One sure couldn't judge a book by its cover.

He drummed his fingers on the steering wheel. If he poisoned the dogs, he could probably get inside the main house through the winery. The lock he'd broken the week before had probably been fixed, but if he'd done it once, he could do so again. Once the dogs were gone.

Maybe he should set the main house on fire. It had been more fun watching them fight the blaze than it would to pick them off like pigeons.

First the dogs, then Deputy O'Connor, then Shea.

He had no problem with Zeke, and even if he did, killing off his friends and the woman he loved would be the highest form of punishment.

David laughed again and increased his speed. His phone rang. He pressed the button on his steering wheel to answer. Amber wouldn't like the fact that he'd set the burner phone up on his Bluetooth, but he didn't care.

"Did you set fire to the vineyard?"

"Sure did. How did you find out?"

"A news reporter interviewed the fire chief. They didn't name you, but who else could it be? Are you squeezing in on my territory?"

His hands tightened on the steering wheel. "The job needs expedited, and you're out of commission."

"I'm healing nicely. Let me do my job." Her tone held a threat. "This will all be over by the weekend. You have my word." She hung up.

He'd make sure of it.

~

"Until the wind picked up, the fire had pretty much stayed on its path." Zeke pulled the collar of his coat higher.

The fire chief nodded. "It would have followed the accelerant trail. You guys were lucky. If it hadn't started to rain…"

Zeke didn't need to be told what would've happened. He wouldn't have lost just his vines.

"The rain will take care of any smoldering embers, but we'll stick around for a bit to make sure."

"Thanks." Zeke returned to the house where he gathered Shea into his arms without asking. Taking comfort from the feel of her would be worth any punch to the jaw.

To his surprise, her good arm snaked around his waist, and she laid her head on his chest. They stood there for several minutes without speaking. His hold on her tightened. She lifted her face to his.

"Do you mind?" He asked softly.

"No. It feels good, and it's been a long, stressful day." Her lips curled into a smile. "Are you going to kiss me?"

He chuckled. "Do you want me to?" He wanted to kiss her very much.

"Yes." Her voice lowered, her breath wafting across his face.

He pressed his lips against hers, softly at first then harder. The kiss burned stronger, brighter, hotter than the fire outside had. He kissed her lips, her neck, every bit of her face until they were both breathless. The kiss held all his emotions—fear, love, desire, worry. When he needed to catch his breath, he pulled back and leaned his forehead against hers.

"Wow." She smiled again, a spark in her eyes. "The way you kiss, it's a miracle you aren't married."

"I don't think I've ever kissed anyone quite that way before." Sure, he'd thought he loved Amber, but not like this all-consuming emotion that grew for Shea. Not the constant fear of something happening to take her away from him.

"Good." She gave him a quick peck that left him hungry for more. "Good night."

"Good night." He watched until she left the room.

"About time," Graham said, entering the kitchen. "The romantic tension between the two of you was about to drive me crazy. I filled the sheriff in on the night's events. He put an APB out on both Real and Amber, although the two are like ghosts." He took a glass from the cupboard and filled it with water. "Sure am glad your vines were saved."

"Me too." He glanced out the window to see the firetruck pulling away. The rain fell steady enough that a constant vigilance wasn't needed.

"I'm not doing a very good job of keeping the two of you safe." He took a long drink from his glass.

"We're still breathing." Zeke clapped him on his shoulder. "We're dealing with two people who aren't afraid of committing murder. It's a miracle we're still alive. Besides, you helped us realize Real is the man Shea came to Misty Hollow to find."

"Thanks, man." Graham finished his water and set the glass in the dishwasher. "See ya in the morning, God willing."

Zeke wouldn't sleep. Not only was he keyed up over the kiss with Shea, but he realized how close they'd come to dying despite the dogs and security system. Why hadn't Real shot them while they were outside? He'd lured them out easily enough. Too easy. All it took was striking at the object of s Zeke's heart.

He pondered Shea's question. They knew he killed her father. Why was he still trying to kill her instead of getting as far away as possible? It couldn't be a pride thing, could it? Revenge for her disrupting his life? It made the most sense. Finish what he'd started.

Did that mean they were dealing with a man who carried a grudge and a woman who enjoyed killing? Other than Amber receiving money, the two would receive nothing after Shea's death.

If it was money she wanted, Zeke had plenty. He could pay her to stop going after Shea.

Chapter Nineteen

The kiss from Zeke the night before had been unlike anything Shea had experienced. She smiled and stretched. The stitches in her arm reminded her she wasn't completely healed. No matter. She would heal, and she would see whether a future with Zeke was possible.

The bigger question was in what capacity? She really wasn't sure whether she wanted to remain a deputy. Shea hadn't chosen the career for the right reasons.

She lightly touched her lips and climbed out of bed. A crisp blue sky greeted her from the window. Thank goodness no rain or snow fell. She'd heard they were experiencing an abnormally cold winter, and she hoped it was over.

Before, she'd been able to see the rental house over the grapevines. Now there was nothing beyond them. The house had burnt to the ground. But, the grape-vines had been saved, and for that she was grateful.

She showered and put her arm in the sling she'd come to hate.

"Good morning." Zeke's smile sent her heart flipping when she entered the kitchen. "Pancakes?"

She shook her head. "Just coffee." She poured a cup and leaned against the counter. "Where's Graham?"

"He had to head to the office for a meeting. We're fine here with the dogs."

At least they'd have a warning if Real or Amber showed, and no one seemed to want the deputy dead. He should be fine. "How'd you sleep?"

"Good. Exhaustion does that for you."

He flipped some pancakes onto a plate and carried it to the table. "Are you sure you don't want any?"

"Positive. I'll gain twenty pounds if I eat like you want me to." She sat across from him. "I might make some toast in a bit. I don't usually eat when I first wake up."

"I like this." He waved his fork between the two of them. "You, me, at the breakfast table. I could get used to you being here."

She could too. "I'll have to go once the danger is past."

"Why?" He forked a bite of pancake into his mouth.

Things weren't as simple as he wanted them to be. "I have some things to figure out."

He studied her face for a minute. His smile faded, then he nodded. "I understand."

Did he, though? She could tell him about her indecision about the future, but why bother him? What if she decided not to stay in Misty Hollow? If she left her job, she wouldn't have many choices in town for work. She'd have to drive to Langley. Too bad she wasn't a sommelier. "I'm starting to feel as if this house is a prison."

"Yeah, I'm going a bit stir-crazy myself. I doubt the sheriff wants us out there, though." He set his fork on the edge of his plate.

She gave a heavy sigh. Even a walk in the cold sounded nice, but that would leave them exposed to two very good shooters. It would be another day of watching TV. At least on the outside. Inside, she'd be working on her plan to persuade Amber to come to her alone. The hardest part would be getting out from under the watchful eyes of Zeke and Graham.

As if he could read her mind, Zeke's eyes narrowed. She focused on her coffee and put on her cop face. If she looked at him, he'd know she was up to something.

The dogs stood then relaxed as Graham entered the house. "Still no sign of Real or Amber." He poured himself a cup of coffee. "This is way better than the slop at the office."

"Another day of doing nothing." Shea stood and set her cup in the sink. "I'm ready to get out of here."

"She's a little grouchy this morning." Zeke tossed her a grin and cleared his plate from the table. "We need to figure out a way of entertaining her."

"Very funny." Shea rolled her eyes.

"I know this will sound cliché," Graham said, "but it's for your own good."

"I know." She headed to her room and plopped on the edge of the bed. The only way to lure Amber out of hiding was to be exposed. She glanced at the bedroom window. It would be a long drop, plus, she wouldn't be able to take the dogs.

The easiest but riskiest way was to simply walk out the back door. That would set off the alarm, but if she hurried, she could be in her car and gone before either of the men reached theirs. It could work. She'd leave that evening once she knew they were both asleep.

With a plan in place, she joined the men in the living room and picked up the remote. "Action and adventure or comedy?"

They looked at her as if she'd grown another set of ears.

"Your pick," Zeke said, sitting on the sofa next to her. He rested his arm along the back, his fingers lightly brushing her shoulder.

It was going to be very hard to leave.

~

Amber paced the floor of the shoddy motel. She'd been a big talker to Real, but she really didn't know what her next step was going to be. Unless she brazenly walked into Zeke's house and started shooting, she had no plan.

That foolish idea would get her killed, and she'd never have the opportunity to enjoy her money and start her new career. If it always took this long to complete a task, she'd run out of money before accepting the next hit.

The deputy needed to be outside where Amber could shoot her sniper-style. That was really the only viable option. How could she coax her into the open?

She chewed her thumbnail and sat on the bed. Being new to town, there really wasn't anyone Deputy Sydney cared about except Zeke. Could he be enticed to meet with Amber, thus causing the deputy to follow? She knew Zeke enough to know that he'd do anything she asked if he thought it would save the deputy.

Her phone rang. It took a moment to realize it wasn't the burner phone. She smiled and answered. "Hello, Zeke. I was just thinking about you."

~

That couldn't be good. Zeke glanced behind him then entered the winery storage room and closed the door. "I have a proposition for you."

"We're way past that." She giggled.

"Whatever David Real is paying you to kill Shea, I'll double it for you to leave her alone."

Silence screamed across the phone for several long seconds before she answered. "You love her that much?" Pain laced her question.

"I think so, yes. Even if I didn't, I'd pay. You should know that."

"Right. Nice guy." Derision dripped from her words. "Unless you're getting rid of me."

He sighed. "You were stealing from the man you professed to love. Did you forget?"

"I needed the money. Now, I've found a way to make a lot."

"By killing people." He leaned his head in his hands. How could he have once cared for this sociopath?

"You have your way; I have mine. I could say, 'sure, you can pay me,' then still kill the deputy."

"You've never lied to me before when I asked you something."

"True. I'll think on it. I did give David Real my word." She hung up.

It was worth a try, but she wouldn't take him up on his offer. Amber might be a killer, but she wasn't a liar. All he could do was hope and pray that she'd think on it and take his money, leaving Shea safe. He'd give her until nightfall to make up her mind. In the meantime, he'd come up with a plan B.

The aroma of baking cookies filled the kitchen as he reentered the main house. Shea had told him she baked when stressed.

He entered the kitchen to see her one-handedly scooping cookie dough onto a baking sheet. "Need some help?"

"I've got it. It's slow going, but it beats watching yet another movie."

"What do you want for supper?" He opened the refrigerator. "We have some steaks. I could grill them."

"In this cold?"

"The steaks won't mind." He grinned.

"Then, that sounds wonderful." She opened the oven and slid the cookie sheet inside. Her words sounded forced.

Why make cookies tonight? She had to have been stressed through all this, but she hadn't baked once since staying in his house. What was she up to?

Fear gripped his heart in an icy fist. Shea had something up her sleeve that he wasn't privy to. Something that could cause him to lose her forever. "I offered to pay Amber to leave you alone." The words vomited from his mouth.

She stiffened then faced him, eyes flashing. "Why would you do that?"

"I can afford it."

"Really? Because I remember you saying it would take some doing to recover from Buford's embezzling. I'm not your girl, Zeke. I'm not someone who needs taking care of."

Ouch. "I thought we were getting close to you being my girl."

"Because of a kiss?" She frowned. "I'm sorry for being upset, but you shouldn't have done that without asking me. We want to catch Amber, not have her flee."

"I understand that, but I'm trying to keep anyone else from being killed." He fell into a chair.

"Drop the nice-guy act for once. Amber and David Real need to be behind bars. That's the goal here." She set the timer on the oven. "Stop trying to fix the world, Zeke. Leave protecting people up to law enforcement." Shea stepped up to him and cupped his cheeks. "I'm sorry about the nic- guy crack. That's what makes you so special."

He leaned into her touch. "I can be not nice if the situation warrants." If it came down to Amber or Shea, he'd be anything but nice.

His phone rang. Seeing it was Amber, he excused himself and stepped outside despite the frigid temperature. "What did you decide?"

"How about you come to me? No money needed. We'll go to Europe together."

"I don't love you, Amber." He sat in an Adirondack chair.

"I don't care. We can still have a great time. I'll make enough money for the both of us."

God help him. Live abroad with an assassin? "Thanks, but no thanks."

"Then things will resume as they are." Her words chilled. "Don't get in my way, Zeke, or you'll suffer the same fate as the deputy." She hung up. He glanced over to see Shea watching him from the window.. He pushed to his feet and went inside to face further lecturing.

Shea removed the cookies from the oven and offered him the first one. "How did she take the news?"

"She doesn't want money; she wants me." He bit into melted chocolate chips and brown sugar. "Oh, this is good." He closed his eyes and savored the taste. "The woman is stark raving mad. Insane. Wants us to go live in Europe together. Bottom line…she will still try and kill you."

"She can try." Shea gave a one-shoulder shrug. "I won't make it easy for her."

After a supper of steaks and salad, the three sat at the table and played a game of gin rummy. Shea seemed distracted, glancing multiple times at the clock on her phone, and went to the restroom more times than was healthy.

Zeke excused himself after Graham received a call about an accident on the interstate and headed upstairs with the pretense of getting a book from his room. He stopped in the doorway of Shea's room. It didn't look as if anyone had slept there in months. Her gun no longer sat on the nightstand. The bedroom curtains were wide open.

"Need something?" She came out of the restroom, drying her hands on a towel.

"Are you okay?"

"Yes, why?"

"Where's your sling?"

"I don't plan on wearing it anymore. My arm is healing nicely." Her smile seemed forced.

His gaze clashed with hers. He'd be sitting up all night to make sure she didn't carry out her plan that meant she was leaving.

Chapter Twenty

Shea lay in bed for several tense minutes to make sure she didn't hear any sounds of anyone awake. The dogs snored from the foot of her bed. No boards creaked, no sounds of the house settling.

In slow motion, she slid to her feet and put on her shoes. She'd slept in her clothes to save time. Shea slipped on her gun holster, then her coat, and snapped her fingers to wake up the dogs.

They leaped from the bed, ready to do her bidding. "Shh, boys."

Shea opened the door, held her breath, then peered into the hall. No light other than what came from the moon and stars. Getting past the guys' rooms would be the tricky part. She wasn't sure if she should sneak past or sprint.

She tiptoed to Zeke's room and held her breath. When no shout came, she peered inside. He rolled over, emitting a soft snore. She used a scarf to tie his doorknob to a wall sconce. It wouldn't stop him, but it would slow him down. Much louder snores came from Graham's room. Shea hurried past and down the stairs.

"We need to run, boys." She sprinted for the front door. The alarm blared the instant she flung it open. Not bothering to close it, she ran to her truck, opened the back door for the dogs, slammed it shut, then climbed into the driver's seat. As she backed away from the house, a shirtless Zeke, struggling to get his coat on, and Graham in the same state of upheaval, stepped onto the porch.

"Stop, Shea." Zeke rushed toward her.

She turned the truck around and sped away, her heart in her throat and tears in her eyes. Would she ever see him again?

Before going to bed, she'd managed to take a look at his phone and memorized Amber's phone number. She intended to call as soon as she lost the tail she knew was coming.

Headlights flickered through the wintry trees. The men were only a couple of curves behind her. She pressed the gas, driving as fast as she thought safe on the mountain road.

The truck fishtailed a few times, but the chains on the tires kept her from sliding too much. Once she hit the bottom of the bottom, she cut down a side road and behind a large building where she dialed Amber's number.

"It's kind of late. Who is this?"

"Deputy Sydney."

"How did you get my number?"

"I stole it. Where do you want to meet? I'm letting you choose so you won't think I'm setting a trap." Shea kept a lookout for Zeke.

"I would have to think about that."

"There's no time. I've left the house, and my partner is searching for me. Either we meet now, or you'll have to find a way to get to me."

Amber laughed. "Sneaky girl. So, you know that

I've been paid to kill you, and yet you still want to meet up with me?"

"Yeah. Let the best woman win and all that." Shea had no intention of fighting or having a shootout. She'd lure Amber out and lay in wait to take her down. She'd most likely lose her job, but it was better than losing her life.

The other woman remained silent for several seconds. "You really want a showdown with me?"

"I want this over." If she lived through it. Shea knew full well one of them wouldn't. "I also want David Real. He needs to pay for killing my father."

"Really? Well, I could slow down on chasing you and go after him if you want to pay me. Then, I could resume with offing you."

"Why would I pay you a large sum of money only to have you return to kill me at a later date?"

"You can't take it with you when you die because you have no family. Your money will go to the state."

The woman was absolutely nuts. "You have ten minutes to make your decision and call me back." Shea hung up on her and turned up the heat in the truck.

Had Zeke and Graham passed her hiding place? Where would they look for her? How long? Knowing Zeke, he wouldn't stop until he'd found her. She really hoped he didn't find her dead, but alive and breathing and standing over Amber. Once the woman was either dead or locked up, Shea would turn her attention to Real. She couldn't focus on him while hiding from Amber.

Her phone rang. "Yeah?"

"Meet me at the rodeo rink, just past the big red barn with more woodpecker holes than not. One hour."

Shea had no idea where that was. "See you there."

She needed to get there before Amber and find a place to take cover. Shea looked up the address with her phone. The closest rodeo rink was forty minutes away.

She frowned. Why did Amber want to meet that far away? Shea set the GPS and pulled away from the building and headed toward the interstate.

Not being a praying woman, she prayed for the first time in a long time as she drove. What she was doing was foolish and reckless, but Shea was tired of being locked in Zeke's house. She wanted her future back—whatever she decided it to be.

Shea made it to the rodeo grounds in thirty minutes. Not seeing another vehicle around, she hoped she'd arrived before Amber and drove around back of a large barn. Several buildings, including an indoor and an outdoor rink, filled the expansive grounds, muddy from the recent snow and rain.

"Here goes nothing, boys." She lowered the windows an inch so they could breathe. "You make sure and bark a warning if you see anyone, okay?" She didn't want them shot trying to protect her, so it was better to keep them in the car.

The dogs whined their displeasure.

"Sorry." She locked the car doors and trudged toward the nearest building. Inside within a large ring were more cows than she could easily count. Several stalls along the edges held bulls and longhorn cattle. The amount of animals kept the room comfortably warm, but the odor almost knocked her off her feet. The noise would effectively hide any sound she would make. The downside was that she also couldn't hear if anyone was near.

~

Zeke had spotted Shea exit the highway and onto the interstate. Keeping two cars behind them, he followed in the old four-door sedan his father had once driven. A car that Shea hopefully wouldn't recognize if she caught sight of them.

"This is the most harebrained thing I've ever seen," Graham said. "I really thought Shea was smarter."

"She wants to end this. Driven by revenge for her father's death, she's not seeing reason." Zeke understood in a way. Shea wasn't a woman to be held down for too long. Cabin fever had forced her hand.

"Well, her plan could get us all killed."

Which is why she tried to sneak away. Separating herself from them was the only way to guarantee their safety. She had to know Zeke wouldn't allow her to take off by herself. Neither would her partner. "Let the sheriff know we're following her."

"Already done. I don't want to lose my job because of this."

Zeke had a strong suspicion that Shea didn't plan on returning to her job when this was all over. It wasn't his place to tell that to Graham. If she quit, the sheriff and the deputy needed to hear it from her own lips.

"She pulled into the rodeo grounds. Aren't they full of animals for an auction?"

"Last I heard." Graham glanced up from his phone. "Pull around back. See if we can spot her."

There was no sign of Shea other than her car. "She left the dogs." A pulse started behind Zeke's right eye. "To protect them, I guess. I don't think Amber would hesitate to shoot a dog, and if Shea had left them behind, they would've barked."

"How did you know she would flee?"

Zeke cut the car's engine. "Her room was too clean."

Graham chuckled. "That's a first. I'll head around the building to the right, you go left. Keep your phone handy." He eyed the gun in Zeke's hand. "You know how to use that?"

"Yes, I just don't like to." Zeke pushed open the car door and stepped out into a night rife with a bitter cold. He pulled the collar of his coat higher and jogged to the nearest building while Graham went in the opposite direction.

The building was teeming with cows. At the far end, Shea ducked into a stall.

Zeke made a move to follow when a blast of cold air hit him in the back. Without looking to see who had entered, he ducked into the nearest stall.

A massive, longhorn cow stared at him, its head down. A quick peek under its belly lessened his anxiety a bit. At least it wasn't a bull. He moved to the back of the stall, using the cow as cover.

Amber moved slowly past, a gun held in her hand and a board in the other. She tossed the board against the wall.

The cow in front of Zeke stirred, kicking up dust. He pinched his nose to hold back a sneeze.

Another mooed, then another as Amber continued toward a door at the far end close to where Shea hid. Zeke slid along the stall wall, then peered through the bars of the door.

Amber stopped in front of the last stall and turned in a slow circle. She glanced at her phone. "I'm on time. Where is she?"

Shea jumped from her hiding place, tackling Amber

to the ground.

Zeke rushed toward them.

Amber punched Shea in the shoulder.

Shea screamed and rolled off her.

Scrambling to her feet, Amber searched for her gun. She grabbed it from inside the stall Shea had exited.

Shea darted into the milling cattle in the pen.

Zeke followed, weaving in and out of the large animals until reaching her side. He grabbed her hand and pulled her after him as he fought to reach the other side.

"You have a gun?" She hissed.

"I had to with the situation you've put us in." A cow turned, hitting him with her rump and smashing him against the railing.

Shea's hand slipped from his. "The cows are starting to panic."

A shot rang out, sending the cattle into a frenzy.

Zeke lost sight of Shea in the confusion. They had to get out of the pen before they were trampled. He shoved against the animal pinning him to the railing. He wanted to shout for Shea but didn't want Amber alerted to her position. Where was she?

A door opened and slammed to his left. He ducked under the railing and headed in that direction. The door led to an office. Another door led outside.

He went through and spotted Graham on the ground bleeding from his head. Zeke felt for a pulse. Strong. He ducked back into the office, found a scarf that had seen better days, and tied it around the deputy's head. "Sorry, pal. Gotta find Shea." Hopefully, the deputy would come to soon. They could use his help.

Back outside, he heard the rumble of a car's engine.

Tank and Beast set up a heavy round of barking.

Zeke peered around the corner to see David Real exit his vehicle. In one hand, he held a rifle.

Zeke needed to find Shea now before the former military sniper found her.

Chapter Twenty-One

Where was she? Amber's palm sweated as she gripped her weapon. Lying law enforcement waiting to pick her off. Wasn't anyone honest anymore?

Amber had been upfront about killing Shea. After all, the woman needed time to get her affairs in order. Now, Zeke had arrived like some stupid knight on a white horse to help her. Did the deputy really need help? Couldn't it be two women vying to see who came out the victor without some guy butting in? Now, she'd have to kill him, too.

She sighed. Guess she'd had that idea the whole time since he wouldn't leave the deputy's side.

It would pain her to kill the man she'd once loved, but work was work. A door slammed on the other side of the pen holding the herd of cows. She sprinted around the perimeter not wanting to get any closer to the smelly beasts' hooves.

Amber moved through an office with a metal desk and beat-up chairs and exited the building. She stopped short at the sight of the male deputy knocked out cold. Since Shea or Zeke wouldn't have been the ones to do the deed, David Real must have arrived on the scene.

She cursed and continued, her ears alert for

movement to lead her to where the others had fled. Why couldn't Real let her do what he'd pay her to do? Or had he come to kill her and prevent her from further bribery?

Ugh. Things had gone from bad to worse in the space of twenty minutes. It seemed as if she were one woman against the world.

~

Shea checked Graham's pulse before alerting the sheriff and asking for backup. Now, she ran through another barn, this one with horses, in hopes of drawing Zeke far enough away from Amber to keep him from being killed.

Having gotten separated in the cow pen, she had no idea where he was, only that he would come looking for her. So would Amber. Shea had to be ready.

Her phone vibrated with a text from the sheriff saying a tractor trailer full of hogs was blocking the road. It was up to her alone to bring down Amber. She prayed she would be up to the task.

"Psst."

She whirled to see Zeke waving her to come his way. He pointed to a side door.

She sprinted toward him, horses nickering as she passed their stalls. Not as loud as the cows, but hopefully they would still muffle any sound.

The room he led her to held tackle and horse feed. He pulled her behind a stack of feed.

"I'm not going to hide, Zeke. I'm going to end this." She started to get up.

"Just until help arrives."

"Which won't be for a long time." She told him about the sheriff's text.

"We could get in our vehicles and lead her to them."

"We can't leave Graham."

"Okay, but David Real is here now. We're up against them both."

A trickle of ice ran down her spine. Why was Real here? Why risk himself when he'd hired someone else to do his dirty work? "He must be the one that blocked the road."

"This is going to be one heck of a showdown."

One that none of them might outlive. Her mouth dried, and perspiration dripped down her back despite the cold. She had so much she wanted to say to Zeke. It had to be now. "If we don't make—"

"Don't talk that way. We *are* getting out of this." He peered around the stack of feed. "I don't like how quiet it is."

She didn't either. The rodeo/livestock auction grounds were massive, but after the rain and snow, their tracks should be easy to find. "I'm not staying here. We're sitting ducks if they do find us."

Shrugging off Zeke's hand, she stood and craned her ears to listen for the scrape of a foot. Not hearing anything, she moved toward the door. The hair on her forearms raised before she touched the knob. Every instinct told her to stay.

She backed up, gun at the ready and waited. After several tense moments with Zeke by her side, she turned the knob and opened the door. Putting a finger to her lips, she glanced both ways. The horses seemed calm, not agitated as when she'd passed them earlier.

A few stirred as she and Zeke moved down the aisle, headed the way they'd come. A door opened somewhere out of sight. They ducked.

"Did you not think I could manage?" Amber's

words cut through the night.

"I've paid you a lot of money. I'm simply here to make sure the task is done by the weekend as you promised," Real's voice.

"Were you followed?"

"No. I blocked the road. It'll take them a few more minutes before any help for the deputy arrives."

"You never did tell me why you want her dead."

"Simply because she's ruined my life with her nosiness."

"Sufficient answer."

A shot rang out.

Shea jerked, meeting Zeke's startled gaze.

"Now that that's out of the way, why don't you come out of hiding? I'm tired of this game," Amber said loud enough for anyone close to the building to hear.

Enough was enough. Shea called out, "I'm here."

"Show yourself."

She caught a glimpse of Amber through the shifting horses. The woman did not have the rifle in her hand aimed in any direction. Instead, it pointed at the ground. Shea strained to see whether her other hand held a handgun. Not seeing one, she got slowly to her feet, her gun at the ready.

"Why'd you shoot Real?" Shea took a step closer. She wasn't close enough to guarantee a shot.

Zeke stepped up beside her, his own gun drawn, a sight that still surprised her.

"Two against one isn't fair." Amber grinned. "So—" she raised her revolver. "Do we just start shooting and hope one of us survives?"

"Sounds like a plan to me." Shea caught a sideways glance of Graham in one of the stalls. "Should we go on a count?"

"Sure. On three. No cheating."

Shea could promise for herself, but what Graham did was something else. "One, two,"

Graham fired.

Amber whirled like a leaf in the wind before falling.

Shea rushed forward and kicked the gun out of her reach. "Just in time, partner. Thanks."

"Is she the one who hit me or Real?"

Shea glanced to where David Real lay. "I'm guessing him. Amber and I have been playing cat and mouse for a while." She pulled a set of handcuffs from the large pocket of her coat. "Hands behind your back."

"I'm shot."

"Not in either arm." Shea glanced at the blood soaking from Amber's coat and into the ground. "We need an ambulance right now."

Graham made the call. "They said they've just cleared the truck. It will be a few minutes." He frowned. "You can tell me what you meant later." He put a hand to where his head bled.

Zeke rolled Amber to her side. "At least the bullet exited. I saw some large rolls of gauze in the storage room."

Shea cuffed the woman and helped her to a sitting position. When Zeke returned with the gauze, she wrapped a thick layer around Amber's middle.

"Why are you helping me?" Amber's eyes widened.

"I swore to serve and protect." Done, she scooted against the wall, her gaze landing on Zeke. She had a lot to tell them once Amber was in the sheriff's hands.

~

Zeke placed horse blankets around everyone's

shoulder and slid down next to Shea. "Glad this is over."

"Me, too."

"Do me a favor." He tilted her chin up. "Don't do anything like this again."

She smiled. "I won't." Something flickered in her eyes that told him she held a secret—one he couldn't wait to hear.

It took a few hours for the scene to be processed. Zeke waited patiently while Shea did her thing. When she finally returned to his side, she wore a smile that hinted at her secret again. "Wanna go home?"

"More than anything." He guided her to the truck, a hand on the small of her waist. Zeke couldn't feel the warmth of her skin through the thick coat, but he had a good imagination.

They weren't even through the front door before Shea stopped him, a hand on his chest. Her gaze settled on his face. "I know what I want my future to hold."

"You do?" His heart stilled.

"I gave my notice to Sheriff Westbrook." Her eyes glittered. "I want to give Misty Hollow a chance to feel like home. I want you to teach me your business so I can help you. I want to work in the winery with you, Nice Guy. I want you. I love you." Tears rolled down her cheeks.

He cupped her face with his hands, wiping the tears away with his thumbs. "I love you, too, Deputy. There's nothing I'd like more than to have you here with me every day running this vineyard and winery with me." He lowered his lips. "I am so very glad you quit your job. I couldn't have handled anymore of that."

"Shut up and kiss me."

He was more than happy to oblige.

The End

Dear Reader,

I hope you're enjoying this little town nestled in the mountains as its people face danger and find love. I know I'm having a blast spending time with my characters.

If you enjoyed this book, I hope you leave a review. Did you miss any books in the series? If not, see the links below. Hope you eagerly await the next book. You can preorder, Say I Don't now.

God Bless,

Cynthia Hickey

Misty Hollow
Secrets of Misty Hollow
Deceptive Peace
Calm Surface
Lightning Never Strikes Twice
Lethal Inheritance

www.cynthiahickey.com

Cynthia Hickey is a multi-published and best-selling author of cozy mysteries and romantic suspense. She has taught writing at many conferences and small writing retreats. She and her husband run the publishing press, Winged Publications, which includes some of the CBA's best well-known authors. They live in Arizona and Arkansas, becoming snowbirds with two dogs and one cat. They have ten grandchildren who keep them busy and tell everyone they know that "Nana is a writer."

Connect with me on
FaceBook
Twitter
Sign up for my newsletter and receive a free short story
www.cynthiahickey.com
Follow me on
Amazon
Bookbub

Enjoy other books by Cynthia Hickey

Misty Hollow
Secrets of Misty Hollow
Deceptive Peace
Calm Surface
Lightning Never Strikes Twice
Lethal Inheritance

The Tail Waggin' Mysteries
Cat-Eyed Witness
The Dog Who Found a Body
Troublesome Twosome
Four-Legged Suspect
Unwanted Christmas Guest
Wedding Day Cat Burglar

Brothers Steele
Sharp as Steele
Carved in Steele
Forged in Steele
Brothers Steele (All three in one)

The Brothers of Copper Pass
Wyatt's Warrant
Dirk's Defense

Stetson's Secret
Houston's Hope
Dallas's Dare
Seth's Sacrifice
Malcolm's Misunderstanding
The Brothers of Copper Pass Boxed Set

Time Travel
The Portal

Tiny House Mysteries
No Small Caper
Caper Goes Missing
Caper Finds a Clue
Caper's Dark Adventure
A Strange Game for Caper
Caper Steals Christmas
Caper Finds a Treasure
Tiny House Mysteries boxed set

Wife for Hire – Private Investigators
Saving Sarah
Lesson for Lacey
Mission for Meghan
Long Way for Lainie
Aimed at Amy
Wife for Hire (all five in one)

A Hollywood Murder

Killer Pose, book 1
Killer Snapshot, book 2
Shoot to Kill, book 3
Kodak Kill Shot, book 4
To Snap a Killer
Hollywood Murder Mysteries

Shady Acres Mysteries
Beware the Orchids, book 1
Path to Nowhere
Poison Foliage
Poinsettia Madness
Deadly Greenhouse Gases
Vine Entrapment
Shady Acres Boxed Set

CLEAN BUT GRITTY Romantic Suspense

Highland Springs

Murder Live
Say Bye to Mommy
To Breathe Again
Highland Springs Murders (all 3 in one)

Colors of Evil Series

Shades of Crimson
Coral Shadows

The Pretty Must Die Series

Ripped in Red, book 1
Pierced in Pink, book 2
Wounded in White, book 3
Worthy, The Complete Story

Lisa Paxton Mystery Series

Eenie Meenie Miny Mo
Jack Be Nimble
Hickory Dickory Dock
Boxed Set

Hearts of Courage
A Heart of Valor
The Game
Suspicious Minds
After the Storm
Local Betrayal
Hearts of Courage Boxed Set

Overcoming Evil series
Mistaken Assassin
Captured Innocence
Mountain of Fear
Exposure at Sea
A Secret to Die for
Collision Course
Romantic Suspense of 5 books in 1

INSPIRATIONAL

Nosy Neighbor Series
Anything For A Mystery, Book 1
A Killer Plot, Book 2
Skin Care Can Be Murder, Book 3
Death By Baking, Book 4
Jogging Is Bad For Your Health, Book 5
Poison Bubbles, Book 6
A Good Party Can Kill You, Book 7
Nosy Neighbor collection

Christmas with Stormi Nelson

The Summer Meadows Series
Fudge-Laced Felonies, Book 1
Candy-Coated Secrets, Book 2
Chocolate-Covered Crime, Book 3
Maui Macadamia Madness, Book 4
All four novels in one collection

The River Valley Mystery Series
Deadly Neighbors, Book 1
Advance Notice, Book 2
The Librarian's Last Chapter, Book 3
All three novels in one collection

Historical cozy
Hazel's Quest

Historical Romances
Runaway Sue
Taming the Sheriff
Sweet Apple Blossom
A Doctor's Agreement
A Lady Maid's Honor
A Touch of Sugar
Love Over Par
Heart of the Emerald
A Sketch of Gold
Her Lonely Heart

Finding Love the Harvey Girl Way
Cooking With Love
Guiding With Love
Serving With Love
Warring With Love
All 4 in 1

Finding Love in Disaster
The Rancher's Dilemma
The Teacher's Rescue
The Soldier's Redemption

Woman of courage Series

A Love For Delicious
Ruth's Redemption
Charity's Gold Rush
Mountain Redemption
They Call Her Mrs. Sheriff
Woman of Courage series

Short Story Westerns
Desert Rose
Desert Lilly
Desert Belle
Desert Daisy
Flowers of the Desert 4 in 1

Contemporary

Romance in Paradise
Maui Magic
Sunset Kisses
Deep Sea Love
3 in 1

Finding a Way Home
Service of Love
Hillbilly Cinderella
Unraveling Love
I'd Rather Kiss My Horse

Christmas

Dear Jillian
Romancing the Fabulous Cooper Brothers
Handcarved Christmas
The Payback Bride
Curtain Calls and Christmas Wishes
Christmas Gold
A Christmas Stamp
Snowflake Kisses
Merry's Secret Santa
A Christmas Deception

The Red Hat's Club (Contemporary novellas)

Finally
Suddenly
Surprisingly
The Red Hat's Club 3 – in 1

Short Story

One Hour (A short story thriller)
Whisper Sweet Nothings (a Valentine short romance)